LEATHER AND LACE

LAUREN LANDISH

Edited by
VALORIE CLIFTON
Edited by
STACI ETHERIDGE

PROLOGUE

ARIANNA

ear Diary,

I'm a whore.

Okay, that's definitely not true. But it might as well be, because that's what everyone thinks of me. I'll admit I've earned that reputation with the biggest con job since Enron.

But it's not all bad. I've gone to all the best frat parties, flirted, teased, and had fun grinding on the dance floor like every college girl should. So everyone just assumes the rumors are true, and I don't say shit to dissuade their thinking.

Reality, of course, is very different. My biggest secret, the one that no one knows, not even my best friend, is that it's all fake.

I'm not a whore. I'm a virgin.

It's a front I chose a long time ago, refusing to play the victim to some stupid high school boy's bragging and society's judgement. As if Mother Nature's gifts of tits and ass were something I should be ashamed of, blamed for. But as I played along as the casual hookup-prone vixen, I realized sex meant more to me. That's when

I decided to save myself for The One. He's out there somewhere, that special man worthy of getting between my legs.

Not that I have time for that right now when all my time and attention are focused on one thing—my career. Well, finishing school and actually having a career, that is. After watching my parents struggle and how they drank their way through most of the meager college fund they'd set aside for me, I want more . . . more than the dead-end, soul-sucking jobs that barely paid enough to make ends meet that my parents had.

I'd hoped my summer internship at Morgan Inc. would be the first step toward that glossy, corner-office future I dream of, especially since it's my first-choice company to work for after graduation. But my hopes of hands-on experience and seeing behind the curtain were quickly dashed, and I've spent the last few months answering the phones and greeting people. I'm willing to work and happy to pay my dues, but my desire for more bubbles beneath the surface every day, pushing me for more, more, more.

And with two weeks left before the end of my internship, I hope I've done enough for them to hire me during the school year. Maybe with fewer interns on staff, I can get that shot at the brass ring and really learn the things I need for my future.

And once I get there . . . then I'll worry about finding Mr. Right.

CHAPTER 1

ARIANNA

"*A*rianna? Arianna!"

I start, sitting up and shaking myself loose from my daydream of me as the boss of a big company, the reality of the plastic chair I'm sitting in mentally replaced by a leather chair in a corner office as I negotiate contracts with other big-wigs.

Checking the clock, I see I've still got a few minutes left on my coffee break. I look up to see Dora Maples standing in the doorway of the small breakroom. It's not fancy—we're first-floor, not the executive level, after all —but the coffee is decent and the vending machine has my favorite afternoon pick-me-up candy bar.

"Yes, ma'am! What do you need, Ms. Maples?"

Dora sets a large manila envelope on the table, sliding it over to me. "I need you to run this upstairs."

"Of course," I quickly reply. Being a delivery girl isn't

usually part of my job description, but I'll take anything that gets me facetime with someone upstairs.

"It's the Iriguchi property papers, with the seal from the county office. Mr. Blackstone needs it on his desk by one," Dora says, squinting and scowling at me as if uncertain I'm capable of a simple delivery. "Run up there and hand it directly to his assistant, Jacob Wilkes. Understood?"

"Consider it done," I reply, picking up the thick envelope and polishing off the last of my morning tea. "I'll do it now."

Honestly, it's probably a blessing she put this errand on me. Jacob Wilkes, Mr. Blackstone's executive assistant, is in charge of the intern program, so I want to stay in his good graces. Even if it's just saying hello and reminding him that I exist, every little bit helps!

The elevator ride feels like an eternity, but I take the time to fluff my hair and smooth my skirt, wanting to look my best for the executive floor and Mr. Wilkes. I knock on Mr. Blackstone's door, but there's no response. After a moment, I gently ease the door open to . . . what the fuck?

It's utter and complete chaos in here. The last and only time I was on the top floor, everything was neat, and while there was a hum of activity, it was organized. This . . . is a loud, crowded clusterfuck of madness, all contained in the vast openness of Mr. Wilkes and Mr. Blackstone's large corner wing.

I stand stock-still for a moment, my eyes scanning as I try to make some sense of what I'm seeing. There is a camera crew set up, complete with lighting, a hair and makeup station nestled in the corner, and a man shouting orders as he rubs roughly at his bald head.

I recognize some of the faces. I helped them sign in when they arrived shortly after eight o'clock for a 'meeting'. I paid attention to them because of the suspicious way they'd refused to explain so I could log them correctly. The only reason I'd let the large group through was because Mr. Wilkes had come into the lobby to escort them up, assuring me it was fine. It doesn't look fine to me though.

I look around for Mr. Wilkes's familiar face so that I can maybe, hopefully, complete my mission, but I freeze when I spot, at the center of the craziness, the sexiest man in the whole damn city, Mr. Liam Blackstone.

I've only ever seen him in person in passing. He flies through the lobby each morning as if he can't wait to get to work, not bothering to acknowledge the peons who sit by the front door, namely me. But he's undeniably the hottest man I've ever laid eyes on. Dark hair fixed in that floppy way that looks casual, but probably took him forever to style, atop an angular jawline that begs to be nibbled. And those eyes! Bright blue that can see right through you or pin you with a stare. Not that he's ever looked at me, but even from the company website, that much is obvious.

The rest of him is just as well put together, lean muscles on his tall frame and an overall aura of 'I'm in charge.' Right now, he's standing in the middle of the maelstrom, a patient, almost amused look on his face and looking like ten million bucks in a custom-tailored pair of black slacks and a slim-fit dress shirt that's open at the neck.

This close, he's nothing at all like the glances I've caught of him as he goes through the lobby. From fifty feet away, he's handsome and sexy. At fifteen feet, he possesses a magnetic aura that seems to envelop the room. He's like a rock star, a general totally in his element, commanding everything in the middle of anarchy.

The slight crunch of the envelope in my hand forces me to pull my eyes away from him. I continue my scan, finally seeing Mr. Wilkes, and walk over. "Mr. Wilkes, sir?"

He barely looks up from the tablet he's poring over, obviously too busy to be interrupted, but I have a mission. "Ms. Maples sent me up with these. It's the Iriguchi property papers?" I hate that I ended that sentence on a lilt, as if I'm unsure. It makes me sound weak, and I'm not. But I am a bit in awe of this whole scene, more fashion shoot than the business meetings I'd expect to see on this floor.

He takes them from my hand, saying, "Thanks." His eyes never glance up to me. So much for facetime with the boss. Feeling the unspoken dismissal, I work my way through the disorder back toward the elevator, only to be stopped when the bald guy freezes mid-tantrum right in front of me to yell at what seems to be his assistant.

The man explodes, "Where is our model!? She was supposed to be here thirty minutes ago!"

The assistant shakes her head, pointing at her phone.

"Francois, Cassie said her flight got delayed. She hasn't even landed yet. It'll be at least two more hours."

I try to discreetly dodge around them, but Francois starts pacing and I back out of the way, not wanting to draw his ire.

"Dammit!" he screams, actually stamping his foot like a toddler. I have to hide my smirk because who does that? He throws his hands in the air. "We'll have to forget the paired shots. Helen's gonna have my ass for this! She specifically asked for sexy couples images," he says before stopping, as if inspiration just struck him. "Wait a minute. Get someone else to take Cassie's place."

The assistant looks aghast, immediately shaking her head. "Francois, I know this is important, but we can't just replace Cassie. There are contracts, consent forms, payments—"

"So what!" Francois interrupts, as if all his problems have evaporated. He snaps, "Get the paperwork started and get out the checkbook. Still cheaper than Cassie's irresponsible ass. Find someone."

The assistant sighs, nodding in defeat but obviously still not quite sure. "But—"

"There." A voice cuts through the noise of the room and everything goes so quiet you could hear a pin drop. I turn to look where the voice came from and am shocked to see Mr. Blackstone pointing at me, his eyes burning into my skin. The nearly feral pull of his gaze freezes me in my tracks. I feel like I'm the prey and I've just been targeted by a predator.

Everyone in the room who'd been curiously watching the exchange between Francois and his assistant is now ping-ponging back and forth between Mr. Blackstone and me. I can feel their eyes, making me hot, the flush of the attention bringing up some painful, awkward memories. Having years of practice is the only thing that saves me from wilting under their judgment.

Still, I'm barely able to utter a squeak as people suddenly start moving toward me, intent on following Mr. Blackstone's orders. "*Me?*" I finally force out, still confused. I clear my throat, getting my voice back to my usual pitch. "I mean . . . me?"

Mr. Blackstone's lips spread into a sexy, cocky grin, and he nods, shooing everyone off as he waves me forward. For some reason, instead of running for my life to the nearest fire escape, my feet move without my even telling them. I walk toward him, my eyes never leaving his.

"Yeah, you," he says. "You look like a doll, perfect and fragile. Sexy and sweet." His eyes caress my face and trace down my body. The body I know has whiplash hourglass curves that make men stupid for no good reason. Usually, I feel defensive when guys look me up and down, like they know something about me just based on my body, but when Mr. Blackstone does it, I feel like standing tall and letting him peruse his fill. His words are probably one of the best, maybe only, compliments I've ever gotten. Maybe that's sad, but it's just my reality. I usually get filthy catcalls and assumptions, not kindness. "You'll do the photoshoot with me."

The photographer lights up like a light bulb. "Yes! She will do. Someone get some makeup on this girl!" His evaluation of me leaves me feeling inadequate, like I don't already look good even though I'm wearing my best daytime, professional look.

But I don't even have time to think about how I'd like to bless him out because Francois's assistant jams a piece of paper into my hands. "Sign here . . . here . . . initial." As she points out each spot to me, she chatters casually. "Haven't you heard? Sexy, young, rich CEOs are all the rage. Books, movies, television . . . it seems that's the recipe for fantasy nowadays!"

"You mean, it hasn't *always* been?" I ask, a hint of sass in my voice before I can catch myself.

Oops. Did I say that out loud? I meant to think that, not actually say it!

"*Cutting Edge Magazine* wanted to do an interview and a photoshoot," Mr. Blackstone explains. "Something about my being the hottest ticket in the business pages, and any press is good press, so here we are." He says it in such a casual manner, like this is all just business as usual for him.

Francois does a little jump and clap before turning to me. "What are you waiting on? Come on, girl!"

That's twice he's called me *girl*. I do have a name, but I'm still too tongue-tied to correct him. "I—I don't know the first thing about modeling," I protest weakly, panicked. "I mean, I'm just an intern here."

Francois waves his hands again. "Don't worry. All you have to do is listen to me and stand beside Mr. Black- stone. *Anyone* could do this next to that man." He gestures outward like it's so easy, snapping his fingers. "Get her ready! We were supposed to be a wrap ten minutes ago!"

The matter seems settled, and before I know it, my hair's been primped, my makeup scrubbed off and a whole new style applied, and they had me change into a blouse that's even tighter across my boobs. I'm nearly shaking, my mind a whirlwind. I came up here to deliver an envelope. Instead, I'm about to take pictures with my boss. My *very* hot boss whom I bet every single woman in this building has a crush on. Awkward.

The assistant appears out of nowhere and leads me over to Mr. Blackstone's desk, where he's sitting nonchalantly, like waiting for this is no big deal. The assistant tells me, "Stand here. Lighting check." And then she disappears, leaving me alone with Mr. Blackstone. Well, not alone, considering there are at least fifteen other people in the room, but it feels like there's a bubble of stillness surrounding us as everyone else bustles about.

"What's your name, doll?" he asks.

Normally, when a random guy goes straight to nick-names and endearments, it makes me grit my teeth. I'd expect my boss doing it would elicit an even stronger reaction. It does . . . but it's not the negative one I'd expect. Instead, I almost swoon. Maybe it's his presence, or the subtle, masculine smell of leather wafting from him, or the way he's staring at me like he already knows my secrets. But there's something in me that likes him calling me that, especially after his earlier compliment.

Calm down, girl. You deal with men like him everyday. He's hot, more than most, but you can control yourself for a few pictures and a fucking conversation that could be your big break.

The reminder that this could be a great career opportunity helps, and I focus as I introduce myself. "Arianna Hunnington. I'm a summer intern, sir."

I offer my hand, which he takes with a smirk. "Liam Blackstone, but I suspect you already knew that." His hand is warm against mine, making me wonder what his touch would feel like on other parts of my body.

Luckily, I'm saved from my own dirty thoughts when Francois comes close. "Okay, you two . . . we want heat for these shots. Naughty girl and the big boss. Got it?"

I can't really say anything else as Francois begins shouting orders as he steps behind the camera. "Let's get this show on the road! Lean into him, girl!"

I hesitate. There he is, calling me *girl* again. "I . . . uh . . ."

Mr. Blackstone is done wasting time though. He takes control, grabbing me by the waist and pulling me into him. "I got you. Don't be shy."

My breasts flatten against him and I throw my head back, trying to get some space between us, but I get caught in his eyes, breathless as I faintly hear a shutter sound. "Yes, yes. Perfect!" Francois crows. "That's it. It's late, and you two are working together when the passion starts to flow between you!"

I barely listen to him. I'm practically melting and these photos aren't even that risqué. I would literally be a puddle on the floor if they were. The feeling of his hard body, even through our clothes, has me so turned on, but at the same time, I'm terrified, too afraid I'll start moaning when he grabs my lower back and pulls me in close. I'm not complaining. I'd do this every day, but what the hell business magazine is this? And what kind of job is this?

Francois notices, scowling. "For God's sake, girl, look like you're enjoying it! I'm sure there's plenty of others around here who'd take your spot in a second!"

Oh, hell no. He's mine. All mine. And equally important, this opportunity is mine, and I'm not going to blow it over some silly school-girl nerves. I've played this part a million times, fooled people better than Francois, and I can do it now if that's what it takes.

So I smile and look up at Mr. Blackstone as innocently as I can despite what's going on inside my head or the desire that's coursing through my body.

"Perfect!" Francois yells. "Now put your hand on his chest!"

My heart pounds, but I play my part, placing my hand on his chest. Oh, my God. Just as hard as I imagined. I want to roam my hand up and down, feel every ridge in his muscles. But he grabs around my wrist, holding me in place, still in charge even though I'm touching him.

There's another series of shutter clicks.

Mr. Blackstone looks down at me. "Put your hand on my thigh."

It seemed different when the photographer was telling me what to do, less personal. But when the demand is from Mr. Blackstone himself, it feels intimate. I hesitate a fraction of a second but obey.

He smirks, giving me a 'good girl' nod.

Oh. My. God. My hand is mere inches from my boss's junk! And I swear . . . no way! He's hard!

"Relax, doll," he whispers, the name between the two of us. "You're about to fall to pieces. I won't bite."

The words pop out before I can think to stop them, flirty and full of my character's sass. "Too bad." His brows lift in surprise at my quick response. Hell, I'm surprised at my comeback too. I try to temper my words and find some semblance of professionalism. "I'm not scared," I protest, faking it if I can't really be sure what the hell I'm doing. "Just not what I thought my work duties were going to entail today."

Mr. Blackstone's grin fades a little and he lowers his lips to just an inch from my ear, his breath sending hot chills down my spine as he whispers, "Your work today involves doing what you're told."

"Hold his belt!" Francois quips, as if he heard Mr. Blackstone's words.

Determined to prove I'm not a scared little girl, I grab his leather belt and give it a tug. I want to look down and get a peek, but I'm not quite that bold. I can feel him, hot and hard, just a fraction of an inch from my hand, so close I can almost feel him.

Francois's murmurs of 'yes' and 'just like that' are getting to me, making me feel like maybe I'm doing okay with this crazy situation, and I find myself starting to get into it, so I swing my foot up, my skirt stretching tight across my ass and thighs, to show off my stiletto heels. Instinctively, Mr. Blackstone reaches down and catches me under the knee, gazing at me with lust in his eyes. I can see the promise of heat in their depths, of things I don't understand, don't know, but I can fake it. I always have. And with him, it's oddly easy to let the desire wash through me, more real than my usual imitation.

We do a couple more shots, but just like that, it's over.

"And we're a wrap! Thank you both!" he yells, clapping his hands. "Now let's get cleaned up and out of Mr. Blackstone's space."

We pull apart, our bodies beginning to get a bit hot and sweaty. My pulse is pounding, and my pussy throbs with every beat of my heart, screaming to be taken. No more waiting. Right now. Mr. Blackstone is the one. Fuck, I've never felt like this. I'm always the one in control of myself, my body, my image. But I feel oddly swept away with him right now, filled with a wild lust I've always scoffed at, but suddenly, it's happening to me.

His eyes are slightly dilated, his cock tenting his slacks as he looks at me, but before we can say anything, I'm ushered away to change out of the magazine's wardrobe.

I'm approached and given a check, two hundred dollars, but right now, I don't care about the money. I just want to get back to Mr. Blackstone. I want . . . more. More of that magnetism, that connection I felt, the look in his eyes when my hand was on his chest or when he cupped the back of my head and stared down at me. I've never felt that rush of attraction, not like that, not that real.

But it must've been one-sided because Mr. Blackstone, for his part, seems to quickly forget about me as he's surrounded by crew. Other than casually reaching down to adjust his cock and get it pointing somewhere other than straight out, I could have disappeared and never existed.

Before I can do anything, I'm quickly shown to the elevator door. I look back, and I see him talking on his phone while directing two other people, and I'm left with a feeling of surrealness. *Did this really just happen?*

CHAPTER 2

LIAM

*F*ucking beautiful.

Naughty perfection.

The angel next door with a dollop of the devil inside.

There are so many ways I could describe the little minx who just left my arms. At first, she seemed so uncertain and innocent, unaware of how my eyes were already tracking her sexy curves from across the room. I'd even had a flash of possessiveness when she'd been speaking to Jacob, who thankfully ignored her. But her nervousness faded away when I took control, and she reared back, rising to the challenge. Feisty minx. That only makes me want more.

Fuck. I'd love to show her what taking control is all about. I want to be the voice in her ear, whispering to the devil inside her that she wants it, even as her better nature is telling her she should run from me. She could run, but the chase sounds exciting, definitely more so than the women who usually throw themselves at me. No, something tells me that Arianna isn't one of those types. She'd make me work for it, earn it, and in return, I'd make her beg.

I was about to ask her more about her time here at Morgan until everyone surrounded me, shoving water in my face, kissing my ass, and generally wasting my precious time. In the few moments it took for me to get rid of them, she disappeared nearly as quickly as she came. Like a mirage, an oasis of beautiful reality in this vast desert of brown-nosing fakers. If not for my hard cock and the pictures Francois is flipping through, I'd wonder if I'd imagined her.

"Do you like this shot?" Francois asks, showing me the initial downloaded shots on his tablet. "I need you to tell me which ones you prefer."

I glance down at the tablet, sighing inwardly because I know my opinion isn't going to matter for shit when Helen gets the images. She'll pick what she wants, my preferences be damned. Not that I care. They're all good shots. "Yeah, go with that."

I still swipe through the rest of them, remembering how she felt so close to me. In each shot, my eyes are drawn to Arianna, the fire in her eyes and the naughty sexuality oozing from her. I tower over her, but she's still powerful, and I have to swallow when I see the image of me holding her leg up. I can actually see a flash of baby blue between her legs. My God, was I that close to her little pussy that her panties could be seen?

"This one," I say, pointing to the shot but covering the space between her legs with my finger. Francois looks over, an evaluative eye scanning the shot as he hums. "Send it to my email now. And then delete it."

He tilts his head. "That's not . . . I can't . . ." He tries to argue, and I'm sure there's some photography code or magazine clause I'm asking him to break, but under the weight of my glare, he starts tapping on the screen. "Done, Mr. Blackstone. Sent and deleted." He looks at me curiously, but I don't have a single shred of intention of explaining myself to him.

I flip through the rest and Francois nods. "Great. I'll get the photo editors on these right away. They might want to have Cassie's head Photoshopped on her body—"

"The fuck? No," I growl, cutting him off. "She stays."

"But—"

I give him a look that says I'm not fucking around, and he goes pale, like he wants to argue but doesn't. "Yes, sir," he agrees, then walks off.

The crew is clearing out, all the fancy equipment that's been cluttering my office disappearing faster than you'd think possible. I'm eager to have my space back to myself so I can get some actual work done today.

Jacob approaches, perching next to me on my desk. He's probably the only person I'd let get away with that. "Hey," Jacob whispers, trying to keep his voice low, "The magazine specifically wanted you with that Cassie chick. She's Instagram famous or some shit, so I don't know if they're going to run it with some random intern on the cover, even if she is hot as sin."

I cut my eyes at him. I want to say something, but Jacob has been my friend and confidant since college and he doesn't mean anything. He's my right-hand man who followed me to Morgan as a package deal. He's the slow and steady brains to my risk-taking gut-following. We're a good team. But right now, I want to knock the shit out of him for even noticing Arianna.

I remind myself to cool it. He's just giving me a heads-up, and Arianna's beauty was apparent to everyone in the room. She's got the looks that make guys want her and girls want to be her, even though she wasn't showy or flashy about it at all. In fact, she might've been trying to disguise it to some degree, her skirt fitting but not too tight, her shirt buttoned over her lush cleavage to be professional, her makeup daytime subtle. It wasn't until the photo crew fixed her up that her bad-girl fuck-goddess was so readily obvious. But I'd noticed her before they'd sexed her up, had already seen beneath the polished surface.

"They'd better, or there won't be a cover. See to it. Arianna's on the cover with me or no deal," I say crisply.

Jacob looks at me in shock but quickly scans my face, reading me like an open book. "Whatever you say. Consider it done." He narrows his eyes, his curiosity piqued, and that's never a good thing. I wait for the interrogation, knowing it's coming. "Anything we need to discuss, Liam?"

"No," I say, not leaving room for further questions. "But I do need one more thing."

"What's that?" Jacob asks, lowering his phone where he's probably already emailing Helen about my stipulations since he's so damn good at his job.

"Find out who Arianna reports to and get back to me."

He's got that look on his face that tells me I'm doing something that he calls 'fuck stupid', but I don't care. "Dude, are you trying to—"

My look silences him, and he sighs. "I'm going on the record now that I'm against *this*, whatever this is. Man, you can't chase pussy around the office. 'Don't shit where you eat' is a saying for a good fucking reason. And an intern? Really, Liam? I can see the HR nightmare coming already."

I glare at him, letting his argument roll right off me. I do what I want and we both damn well know it.

He clenches his jaw, and I know I'll hear more on this, but for now, he gives in. "All right, I'll get that for you as soon as possible. You put me in charge of the interns anyway. It's in my office somewhere."

"Good. And tell them to hurry up and clean this place up. I want work back to normal here in an hour."

Jacob leaves, and I settle in my chair, one thing and one thing only on my mind.

Getting Arianna in my arms again.

AFTER THE PHOTOSHOOT IS OVER, WHIRLWIND ONLY begins to describe the rest of the day. I quickly get bogged down by work and two conference calls, and I temporarily forget about what happened earlier.

Temporarily.

Now, as the last glow from the setting sun fades to deep purple in the west, I can't stop thinking about her as I sit in my office, my back turned to the door while I watch the city from the floor-to-ceiling windows that give me a commanding view of downtown.

Those brown eyes. That smile. The way her tits felt pressed against me . . .

My thoughts of Arianna are interrupted by my phone ringing, and I turn away from the skyline, my cock yet again hard in my slacks. It's probably the worst time for a stiffie, considering whose customized ringtone, Avicii's *"Hey Brother"*, is playing on my phone.

"Hey, big bro!" my little sister, Norma Jean, chirps sweetly. Just turning twenty this year, she's the most important person in my life, even if she does push all my buttons sometimes. It's not her fault she's still wearing little girl blinders about our asshole of a father— although he's admittedly been a kinder parent to her than he ever was to me, something I think Norma Jean's mother had a heavy hand in. Maybe if my own mother had been stronger, I would've had a different father-son relationship with him too. But that ship sailed long ago.

"Hey, NJ!" I say. "What's up? I'm a little busy."

"Oh, please." Norma laughs. "I know your schedule.

You're almost done with work and were probably looking out the window while considering your kingdom and coming up with your next plan to take over the world."

Damn, she's good. Still, I can't let her know she pegged me exactly right. "I'm never done with work. You know that. And my kingdom is everything the light touches . . . everything," I say in a wise voice. I must've watched The Lion King with her a hundred times when she was young, and I'd wager that she still watches it pretty often, even if we don't sit down and marathon watch movies together anymore.

"Slick quote usage, Liam." I can hear the smile in her voice as she remembers those nights curled up on the couch too. Back then, I'd been barely a teenager and she'd been the toddler little sister my father had sprung on me with his new wife, my stepmom. I'd never felt like I was being replaced simply because I'd never felt like I'd had a place in my dad's heart to begin with. But Norma Jean did then and still does. Her sweet laughs and strong will had let her worm her way into my heart all too easily back then. "So, Mr. Busy, what did you do today?"

I secretly love when she does this, call just to catch up. Everyone else wants something from me. She just wants to chat. It's a rare treat for me. "Oh, a bit of this, some of that, some conference calls, a photoshoot and inter-view, a few contracts. The usual."

Just as I gleefully expected, she screams, "A photoshoot and interview?!? What the hell, Liam? Tell me all about it. You know I live for that stuff."

"I know. But it's hush-hush, top-secret, okay?" She hums her agreement, so I tell her all about the interview with *Cutting Edge*, making sure to give all the details I know she wants.

She sighs blissfully. "One day, that's going to be me. I'm going to be sitting in penthouse offices, interviewing bigwigs, and finding out what makes them tick. I'll get all the low-down dirt on the country's biggest companies. And then maybe politicians too—that's where the real gritty stuff is."

I can hear her excitement, her passion, and I smile at how similar to me she sounds. We're both driven to the point of near-obsession, and we get what we want ninety-nine percent of the time. "You'll do it too. Get your degree, work your ass off, and you can do anything, Norma."

"I did apply for a job at the university newspaper. It's really competitive, and they mostly only hire seniors, but my interview went really well. Even if I get it, it'll probably be small human-interest stories for a while, but it's a start. Cross your fingers for me."

I recognize that this is a big deal for her, a reach for something she really wants but isn't sure she's ready for. But I know she can handle it. "You don't need crossed fingers or luck, Sister. You are ballsy and brave and have more brains than just about anyone I know. You'd be a perfect journalist for a hell of a lot more than puppy adoption stories, and they'll see that. So swallow those nerves and go get what you want."

It's my version of a pep talk, more 'work for it' and less 'you deserve it' because I'm well aware we don't always get what we deserve, but we damn sure get what we work for.

"Thanks, Liam. That means a lot, especially from you. I tell you what. When I get hired, I'm going to interview you and do an insider's look at the country's hottest CEO."

I notice she didn't ask but rather told me, and I smirk at her assumption. Big clanging balls on that girl. Nobody tells me what to do, except her . . . and sometimes Jacob.

As if my thoughts conjured him, Jacob steps in, and I hold up a finger, having him pause. "Listen, gotta go. Keep working hard and nothing's going to stop you. Love ya."

She responds in kind, and I hang up, turning my attention to Jacob.

"She's a college student. Summer internship," Jacob says quickly, setting a file on my desk. I run my thumb along the label . . . *Arianna Hunnington*. "She'll be gone in two weeks until next semester . . . assuming we bring her back."

I tap my fingers on the file, quickly fingering out a quick little rap beat as I think. Two weeks to make her mine.

Or to make her stay.

Either way . . . I'll have my way.

"I can almost see the dirty thoughts running across your

face and I'd like to reiterate my stance that this is a bad fucking idea. A human. Resources. Nightmare. With a side serving of PR shit show for the company you're supposed to be taking into the next market wave. Liam?" Jacob asks harshly as I finish my beat.

"I want her moved up here," I declare, turning to him and completely tuning out his reasoning. He's right, he almost always is, but I don't care this time. "Starting tomorrow, she'll be my secretary."

"Huh?" Jacob asks, confused. "She's just a college intern. And in case you didn't notice, you don't need a secretary. You have an executive assistant. Me."

"Well now, I'll have a secretary too. It's not like you can't use a little assistance from time to time."

Jacob shakes head. "There are protocols we have to follow. You can't just move her up like that."

That's Jacob. If he can't get me to listen to reason, he'll try another tactic. He learned that from me, and he is always a stickler for the rules. "Such as?"

"Well, she'd have to be interviewed."

"Fine. I'll conduct it myself."

Jacob shakes his head. "You can't just interview her yourself! There are rules—" Jacob stops when he sees my expression. He should already know I'm going to get what I want. And I want her. "Fuck it . . . we'll interview her together. Satisfied?"

He sighs and nods but gives me a hard look.

"Get her up here," I growl. "Now."

"Now? She may have already left for the day," Jacob reminds me as he looks at his watch. "You know, most people go home about an hour ago."

He's got a point. "Tomorrow morning then. First thing."

 *ear Diary,*

I CAN'T BELIEVE WHAT HAPPENED TODAY. I MEAN, GOING upstairs to deliver some papers to the top floor was already exciting, but to then be picked out of the crowd and pulled into a photoshoot with Liam Blackstone?

Holy Fuck, that man is sex in a suit. He's an alpha in every sense of the word, people scurrying to do what he says, not because he's wealthy or the boss but because he has this air of dominance. I've never felt anything like that before, the weight of his very presence effortlessly drawing my attention and tuning my body into his.

I'll admit that the feeling of being pressed against him, his cock hard on my ass, was shockingly erotic. The desire and surprise in my eyes as I looked over my shoulder at him weren't pretend like usual. And I'd had a weak moment when we'd separated where I wanted more, wanted it all, had even considered for a moment that he might be The One, considering the way he made me feel. But that's a danger zone I don't need to venture into . . . no sex, not now. Not until my career is on target and I find the right man, preferably in that order.

But there's no harm in fantasizing, and I definitely did that as soon as I got home, touching myself to the thoughts of his hands on my body, his whispered words hot in my ear, his thick cock taking my pussy for the first time.

THE NEXT MORNING, I'VE BARELY WALKED IN THE DOOR before Dora is riding me. She follows me into the breakroom, and as a peace offering, I make her a coffee while she complains about the time I spent away from my desk yesterday. "I had to pull another intern from her duties to cover for you, so you'll be returning the favor to her today and handling her tasks."

I nod, not interrupting her tirade as I hand the steaming mug over, made to the exact specifications I know she prefers, and she accepts it without a single word of appreciation. I turn back around to make my own cup of caffeine nectar, wishing I could have something stronger to make dealing with Dora a bit easier. I wonder if there's an espresso machine on Mr. Blackstone's floor?

"Your to-do list is on your desk so you'd best get started because I expect it to be complete before you leave today. You'll need to stay on task today, Ms. Hunnington." Dora huffs at me with a stern look.

"Of course, Ms. Maples. I did complete the tasks you assigned me yesterday. I apologize if the change in plans once I got upstairs left you short-handed." It takes everything I can to apologize to her, especially since I know I didn't do anything wrong. When the CEO tells you to do something, you do it, and she damn well knows that. But she's getting too much evil joy out of putting me in my place.

"Hrrmph. You'll be staying behind the front desk today, that's for sure, because apparently, you can't be trusted to complete a simple delivery task upstairs."

I nod. "Yes, ma'am."

Someone clears their throat from the doorway and Ms. Maples and I both turn to look. "Excuse me. Ms. Hunnington?"

It's Jacob Wilkes, looking like he'd rather be anywhere than here. Speaking of, why is he here? The ground-floor coffee room isn't exactly his area of the building.

Dora looks at me with smug glee in her eyes, and I realize that Mr. Wilkes is not just looking *at me*. He's looking *for* me, which can't be good. "Yes, Mr. Wilkes?" I force myself to stand tall, refusing to wilt like some mild-mannered nitwit. If I'm getting fired for doing that photo shoot yesterday, I'll be pissed since Mr. Blackstone is the one who demanded I do it in the first place. "Can I help you?"

He scans me up and down, not creepily but almost analytically, and then sighs. "I need you to come with me, please." He turns. "Dora, I overheard your assignment and I'm afraid Ms. Hunnington won't be at the front desk today. Please reorganize staff as you see fit."

She dips her chin, and I swear I can see her fighting the urge to fucking curtsy. "Of course, Mr. Wilkes. I have several other interns who are more than qualified to do what Ms. Hunnington isn't able to do." The dig is sharp and hits home, just as she intended.

Mr. Wilkes doesn't respond, just tilts his head at me, silently telling me to follow him. And like a damn puppy, I do, following him obediently across the foyer to the elevator, watching as he pushes the button for the top floor, and down the hallway to Mr. Blackstone's office.

"Wait here, please," Mr. Wilkes says after seating me in the plush leather chairs now rearranged in front of the desk. The click of the door closing sounds like a gunshot, right to the heart of my career. Dead before it even really started.

I feel like I'm a bag of silverware. Everything is jangly as my nerves go into overtime and my mind races through possible scenarios. Why am I here? Is it about yesterday? Was Mr. Blackstone as hot for me as I was for him?

Hold up, let's hit the brakes right there . . . that's only in my dreams. More likely, I'm about to get fired from my internship and lose any chance at a good reference or post-graduation job I might've had.

All my thoughts black out at that, the pit in my stomach sucking down all my hopes like a vortex, and I go vacant. My eyes mindlessly float around the room and I get my first real view of the CEO's office without the photoshoot madness. It's spectacularly opulent, with floor-to-ceiling windows that give a great view of the western skyline of the city. Right now, the shades are half-pulled and the sun's starting to peek through the upper windows, but still, the view is breathtaking.

The rest of Mr. Blackstone's office is just as tremendous and screams *him*. Rich, dark brown leather chairs sit in front of a huge oak desk. Behind it is another leather chair that looks damn-near like a throne, and the walls are lined in oak bookshelves.

After a minute that seems like an eternity, the door opens once again as Mr. Blackstone comes in, followed by Mr. Wilkes. I'm not sure if I should sit or stand, but I take the safer approach and rise, offering a hand. "Sir, you wanted to see me?"

He smiles subtly as he shakes my hand, the formality awkward considering how physically close we were just yesterday in this very room. "Have a seat, Arianna," he says, not turning around. "Jacob, you may go."

"We were supposed—" Jacob starts, then nods at the sharp look he receives. "Of course."

I don't have time to wonder what that was about as he leaves, closing the door behind him. Mr. Blackstone gestures to the chair behind me. "Please . . . have a seat."

I smile a little and sit down. "Thank you. I hope everyone was pleased with the shoot?" I'm fishing, trying to suss out why I'm here without asking outright.

To my surprise, he doesn't walk to his throne-like chair to sit, instead choosing to sit in the guest chair next to me. I get a whiff his cologne, or maybe that's just him . . . musk and leather and spice. He smells like power.

"Oh, yes . . . definitely," he replies, more professional and formal in his speech than yesterday, but dancing underneath is still the cocky bastard who whispered in my ear and spent last night invading my dreams. I don't know what the sudden change is about. Perhaps he realized he was being unprofessional and wants to reestablish that level of things.

My confused expression seems to say it all, though, and he chuckles. "I was actually rather impressed with your ability to adapt to the high-pressured situation, roll with the punches, if you will. I wonder if you are usually so adept at doing what you're told?"

The compliment is tied up in innuendo, and I'm getting whiplash from his switches between professionalism and definitely not-professional. "Thank you," I hedge. "I enjoy working at Morgan and was willing to take one for the team to insure a positive result for the photoshoot. I'm glad my work was to your liking." And like a hot knife through butter, I use the same tactic on him as well, mixing a small hint of naughty into my formal words.

He smirks, seemingly enjoying the back and forth play, then leans forward, placing his elbows on his knees. "Let's cut to the chase. I'm hiring a secretary and you're here to interview for the position."

I'm pretty sure my chin hits my knee. Is he fucking kidding me? His secretary? That's like a fifty-step leap from where I currently sit, and that gig ends in just two weeks. This could be a dream come true. This could be the start of everything. "Uhm . . . but . . . sure."

His smirk grows as he revels in my brain's apparent shutdown. "Take a deep breath, Miss Hunnington. I'll get you a drink."

At first, I think that he's going to get me a scotch or something from the small minibar on the side of the room that he goes over to, even though it's barely mid-morning, but when he comes back with a clear glass of soda water with a twist of lemon, I'm relieved. This is a real opportunity and I'd better take advantage of it.

He sits down across from me, crossing his legs and considering me while I take a sip. "Better?"

I nod and uncertainly hold the glass, not sure where to set it. He takes it from my hand and places it carelessly on his desk, definitely not something I would've ever done. "Thank you, Mr. Blackstone. I appreciate the opportunity. But might I ask . . . isn't this irregular? To consider me for a position as your secretary when I'm a front desk intern?"

Shit. I sound like I don't want the job. Of course I want it! But it does sound too good to be true, which in my experience is a definite red flag.

Liam chuckles, shaking his head. "You and Jacob. He'll like you. As to your question, I'm the boss and I can do what I want. I make the rules around here."

I sit up straighter in my chair, squaring my shoulders. "Of course, sir. Can I ask why me? As far as I'm aware, you didn't know I existed before yesterday."

He nods. "As I said, you handled yesterday's situation well. Tell me about yourself."

I lift an eyebrow, not sure how to take this. Shit, maybe I impressed him even more than he impressed me.

Wait. No, that's not possible. But if this is real, I need to get my head in the game, because a chance like this doesn't come around more than once.

"I'm a junior at the university, with a 3.83 GPA, majoring in international business with a focus in negotiations and contracts. My previous internship was with Orion Industries, where I mostly acted as a third set of eyes on contracts, learning the appropriate wording for their various industry-specific clauses. This year, I set my sights on Morgan Inc. as my first-choice internship and was fortunate enough to be tapped for the program. I've been working with Ms. Maples on the first floor, primarily as a receptionist, greeting visitors and answering the phone." I try to give him as much insight as I can while still being concise.

He nods. "And do you feel your time here has been beneficial?"

It sounds like a trick question. In fact, I'm rather sure it's a trap, so I tread carefully. "I do. While the work itself has been easier than my previous internship, seeing the inner workings of Morgan has been extremely valuable and I hope to continue here with part-time employment in the fall when I return to my full course load." Bob and weave the hazard and slam-dunk the request.

"What was the most difficult job you ever had?" he asks.

"This one might surprise you. Working at the Dairy Queen as a teenager." His eyebrows lift, just as I expected. "No, really. It was my first job, so I was nervous, and I had to take orders on a headset that cut in and out randomly, ensuring that approximately every fifth customer was mad as hell by the time they got to the window. I also had to make change without a calculator, fill orders in a timely manner, and clean the ice cream machine every night." I shiver for effect. "That thing was so gross, I could never eat ice cream again."

He grins. "That actually does sound pretty bad. Where do you see yourself in five years?"

These questions seem like Interviews 101, so maybe this is actually real. I start to get more hopeful. "Maybe closer to ten, but I'd like to be the CEO of an international firm, sitting somewhere like you are now," I state proudly.

"Ambitious. I like it," Liam says before grinning. "But it takes a lot of sacrifices to make it where I am."

I nod. "It does, but I'm willing to work hard. I have been for years and don't foresee that changing. I enjoy the challenges of business, how each new product or contract offers something totally unique and new."

He strokes his chin for a moment, and a new light comes to his eyes as he gazes at me. He's not looking at me professionally anymore, but like he did yesterday. I swear the temperature in the room just jumped a few degrees. "Now I'm going to ask you some questions that are totally off-record. If they unnerve you or offend you in anyway, you can get up and walk out that door and never come back. You'll get a letter of recommendation for your internship regardless of what you decide. But I assure you, the last thing you want to do is walk out that door."

Now what in the world could have him saying something like that? It's like he's still maintaining power, but he's not beating me over the head with it. I nod my head slowly, leaning forward in anticipation of where this is going. "Ask away."

Liam also leans forward, almost halving the space between us, and I feel the power in his body calling to me and my body responding. My pussy tingles, and I can feel my nipples starting to stiffen in my bra. "Tell me, doll, when's the last time you masturbated?"

What the actual fuck?! Leave! Just get up, walk out that door, and take the first elevator you can back down to the first floor. You don't need this! my mind seems to scream. *I knew this was too good to be true, and he's just like every other asshole, even if he's the only one to ever make my body respond the way it did yesterday. I'm worth more than this shit.*

I stand, looming over him intentionally for what I have to say. I know my eyes are blazing fury and I want him to see every bit of that fire. "That is none of your business, Mr. Blackstone. I thought this was a serious job offer, and while you may think I'm the weaker player in this little back and forth chess game we've had going here, I assure that I am not some silly little girl awed by your audacity and arrogance. Contrary to some people's opinions, I'm not some whore, and I won't let you string me along, lording some false opportunity over me when what you really want is something much baser. I'm sure you can get that elsewhere."

I am dying inside at the loss of what I thought was going to be a real opportunity, the hope that had already started burning sparking out in a flashbang, leaving only the smoke to obscure my eyes. I'm proud of myself for standing up to his rude question, but the tears are already burning behind my eyes as I walk toward the door.

"Stop . . . wait." He says the command in a hard voice, and despite my desire to get out of here, he is my boss, and on some level, I think I'm hoping he'll apologize for the gross misstep.

I stop just shy of the door, and he gets up, stalking toward me. Unable to stop myself, I shrink and my back presses to the door. Though he doesn't cage me in with his arms, I feel just as trapped by his gaze, frozen as he stares down at me. "Did I misread you yesterday, Arianna? Did you enjoy the photoshoot with me?" His voice is softer, kinder, though still demanding.

I'm still mad as hell, but another side of me, the part that remembers how it felt being pressed against him yesterday and is experiencing the same buzz from his proximately now, is turned on, keeping me rooted in place. But I still call him out, refusing to back down. "You already know you didn't misread, but your question was way out of line."

He dips his chin. "My apologies then." He says the word as if he's tasting it, like a rare delicacy he's never experienced. I have a feeling that's true. He doesn't seem the type to apologize for much, so I nod back, silently and graciously letting him know I accept.

It feels like a reset of the chess board, like he's looking at me as something greater than a fucktoy intern to use for shock value and good times. It's a damn good thing, too, because I am more than that. But the dance begins again, more tactfully this time.

"Not to reignite your ire, but you said, 'contrary to some people's opinions'. What did you mean, Arianna?"

I can tell he's broaching carefully, and I respect his diplomacy for asking that way, but it's not a story I usually share. But something makes me want to tell him. Maybe it's the patient way he's waiting right now, not pressuring me, even though I know he desperately wants the story. It doesn't feel salacious but more that he wants to know my details. I let my eyes drop, not able to look him in the eye as I whisper my confession. "Not that it matters, but once upon a time back home, I went out with a boy. He bragged big and loud about things that didn't happen. It became a thing, and at some point, folks decided 'the lady doth protest too much' and began to tease me mercilessly. So I took control, embraced what they thought, even if they were wrong, and used it to my advantage. It's a part I've played well and often as it suited me, even if it's not the truth."

"And what part is that?" he asks, though he knows the answer.

I realize he wants me to say it. I lift my chin, meeting his eyes directly, and I find the strength in my core that I always need for this. "A whore."

He grins ferally at my use of the filthy word, like he likes it. His eyes bore into mine, lengthening the heavy moment and making me feel exposed, and though I'd die before admitting it, turning me on. The heat of my anger is morphing inside me, fraying around the edges and curling into an almost painful need. I can feel the weight of him even without actual contact, as if my skin yearns to touch his. This is what I felt yesterday, but amped up so much more.

"If I don't ask you questions, can I tell you what I know, Arianna?" he whispers huskily.

I bite my lip but give the slightest of nods.

His delight at the victory is in the tilt of his lips. "I know that you are a brilliant woman with a mind for business. I know that you are capable of speaking your mind, even when it borders on dangerous. I know that you see possibilities where others see risk." His eyes dip down before lifting to meet mine once again. "I know that your nipples are hard. I know that your pussy is wet for me. And I know that my cock is throbbing for you."

Everything he said is true, both the mental compliments and the physical realities. He steps closer, and I can finally feel the searing connection of our skin. It's heavenly bliss but also hell because it's so fucking hot. I vaguely wonder if it's this hot through the filter of our clothing, would our naked bodies would simply spontaneously combust on contact? My pussy clenches at the thought, and I barely hold back the whimper in my throat.

"So tell me, Arianna. You may not be a whore, but what

are you? Are you a woman who wants to see where this might lead, what's behind door number one?" He places his hands on the door behind me, one on either side of my head, caging me in. "Or are you a woman who wants to play it safe? Tell me, doll."

At first, I don't say anything, truly contemplating my sexual choices for the first time in years. I made a decision a long time ago as a girl, in response to other's critiques, but I'm different, stronger now. Or maybe I'm weaker, because he definitely makes me consider giving in and just bending over his desk so he can take me. The sexy image makes my breath hitch, and I know he's scanning my face, looking for any hint of my thoughts.

At the last instant, a quiet little voice inside me whispers, lending me strength. *Remember, you're saving yourself. You don't need to sell yourself short.*

Liam tilts his hips against me, and I can't help but moan softly, my eyes rolling at the grinding pleasure. Liam quirks an eyebrow, and I clear my throat. I shouldn't tell him. Nobody knows, not even my best friend, Daisy. But I can't help myself.

With the last shreds of my strength and confidence, I place my hands on his chest and look him in the eyes. "I'm not a whore. I'm a virgin."

CHAPTER 4

LIAM

"*I*'m a virgin."

The words hit me with the power of a super-charged lighting bolt. This sweet, sexy little angel in front of me is a virgin? Pure and untouched? You'd never know it with how flirty she is. Yesterday, she played with me like a kitten with a string.

She's almost breathless, aroused at my question, and I can see the tremulous pride in her shoulders. She's been hiding it, pretending to be the flirty little vixen. But she wants me to fuck her, even if she doesn't fully realize it yet. I can see it in her eyes.

"Are you telling me the truth, Arianna?" I hiss, still a seed of doubt in my head as I wonder if this is a game she's playing.

She nods, more confident this time. "Yes." And I see the raw honesty of her answer.

I bite my lip to hold in the groan but lean back a bit,

43

letting my cock tent my pants and doing nothing to hide it. Let her see what she does to me. We both know she wants it. "Yes, sir," I correct her.

"Yes, sir," she repeats, looking at me through her lashes. "I've never had sex before."

"That's hard to believe," I challenge her. "You were very convincing yesterday."

"It's the truth," she says before her confidence falters. "I don't know why I'm telling you this. I've never told anyone." I can see the thought of running blooming in her eyes, and I circumvent her.

I press back closer, not touching her but just shy of it as I lean to her ear, letting the quiet of my whisper soften the filthy words I say to her. "You've never even had a man eat that sweet little pussy? Felt his fingers plunge into you until you were fucking his hand?"

She squirms a little, and I can tell she's thinking about it. "No. I've never even touched a man's dick before." My own cock jumps at the words on her lips, but I ignore it for the time being, keeping my focus on Arianna and the things I could do to her, make her feel.

"And would you like for me to give you that opportunity? To show you what it feels like to have my tongue dance on your clit until you scream in ecstasy . . . before I sink first my fingers and then my cock in that virgin pussy?"

She squirms more, a flush coming to her cheeks, and she looks so fucking sexy. I'm feeding the naughty side of her, tempting her, teasing her. We both want it. She just has to say yes.

"It would be inappropriate," she manages, her breathing heavy. "On so many levels."

"I'm an inappropriate person on so many dirty, wonderful levels," I retort with a grin. Fuck, I can almost picture sucking on her pretty pink pussy. I'd have her chasing my tongue and begging me to never stop. "Are you sure?"

"I–I–I'm saving myself," she admits, looking down into her lap.

"For whom?" I ask, interested. Is she dating someone? He must be a weak asshole if he hasn't claimed her yet. More importantly, she must not want him if I can push her buttons so easily, and yet she seems so surprised by her body's every response. I want these breathy sighs for my own, her orgasm at my hand, no one else's. Just mine.

Arianna whimpers again, biting her lip. "The perfect man. My future husband."

Oh, my sweet doll . . . so innocent. And so sexy. "I don't know if the perfect man exists, but there's a man who can make your eyes roll back in your head, a man who can make you scream so hard you forget who you are, a man who can make you want to be fucked so badly that you'll do anything to have it."

Her chest is heaving, her eyes almost glazed over as her lip trembles, and if I pushed the issue . . . I could have her now. "And you know who that man is?" I growl, leaning back. "That man is me."

But I realize I want more than just a quick fuck in my office. I want more than her cherry. I want her everything. It's been so long since I had to chase, to earn it . . . and when I do, it'll be so much sweeter.

She's quivering, practically shaking in her skin. "Mr. Blackstone . . . Liam . . . sir . . ."

No, my sweet little doll. It's not going to be that easy. Not for either of us.

I trace my fingertips down her cheek and along her jawline. She lifts her chin unconsciously, seeking my lips, but I hold back, teasing us both and letting it build. "Do you feel that electricity shooting through you, Arianna? Just from my touch along your silky skin?" I let my fingers drift lower with my words, from her neck down to her collarbone.

She arches her back in answer, not realizing what she's begging for, but I take advantage of the shudder that rushes through her, leaving the relative safety of her shoulder and dropping my hand to her thigh. I grab a firm handful, letting her know I'm there before caressing up to her ass.

"This ass pressed against my cock drove me wild yesterday. You may not have answered the question, but I will. I jacked off last night to thoughts of you, your dark hair twisted up in my fist as I plunged into your hot pink slit, the feel of your slick wetness coating me in your cream. I pumped my cock, rock-hard for you, up and down . . . up and down . . ."

I trail off, realizing that she's working her hips along me with my words, mimicking what I say. And though it feels amazing, and I could come from that alone right now, this is about her, not me. I want to make her come like she never has before, pressed right against my door and under my hand.

Her rocking motion has inched her skirt up her thighs, and now I can feel more of her heated flesh. I let my fingers roam higher too, until I feel the lacy edge of her panties. I growl when I discover how soaked she is. "Fuck, doll. You're dripping for me. I'm going to be the one who fills this sweet virgin pussy first."

She tenses slightly but doesn't resist. I want her at ease, though, so I reassure her. "Not today, not like this, but soon, you're going to be begging me to fuck you, to fill you with my fat cock."

I almost expect her to sass back with some sharp retort, but a glance at her face tells me that she's far too gone for thoughtful dialogue. Her mouth hangs open, panting for breath, and her eyes are closed, lost to the new sensations I'm piling onto her body.

I dip a finger inside her panties, getting instantly covered in her honey, and let my finger run from her opening to her clit and back, slow and easy so she doesn't spook. She cries out, and I cover her mouth with my own, silencing her pleasure with a kiss.

Her hands weave into my hair, pulling me into her, and she kisses me back passionately. Our tongues tangle as we devour each other, sharing breath and space with the ease of long-time lovers and the fire of first-time fuckers.

I pull back, needing oxygen and needing her. Meeting her eyes, I tell her, "Another time, another place, I'm going to have you screaming my name to the heavens above. I'll teach you that heaven is being impaled on my cock and riding me until your heart feels like it's ready to explode. But this time . . . you have to be silent."

She nods but finally finds herself enough to speak. "Mighty confident in yourself, aren't you?"

I smirk, glad she's with me and not wholly lost to the waves of pleasure sweeping her body. "You have no idea, Arianna. I have a deal for you. Let me touch you, show you that I can give you pleasure you've only dreamed of. I promise I will let you walk out that door still a virgin, but one who knows the amazing things her body can do."

She's bucking her hips against the air, searching for something she doesn't understand yet. Suddenly, she freezes and narrows her eyes at me. "And the secretary job?"

Smart girl. Good girl.

Her brains turn me on even more than her body, if that's possible. I take her chin in my hand, forcing her eyes to mine so she sees me clearly. I growl, "*This* has nothing to do with *that*. You are not a whore, Arianna, and I never thought you were. I think we both know that job was yours when you walked in the door this morning. And this—us, one way or the other—doesn't change that for you." I want her to come to me freely, to want me and want what I can do to her, not want what I can do for her career. She seems to feel the same way and is soothed by my blunt words.

"Yes, Liam . . . sir. Please." Her sweet surrender, the breathy sigh of her acquiescence, is music to my ears and dynamite to my lust.

I drop my hands to the hem of her skirt, lifting it so it bunches around her waist. The first sight of her panty-covered pussy has my cock throbbing so hard I have to squeeze it to stop myself from coming. She's soaked through, red lacy panties that are so naughty . . . but I know what's underneath is untouched. Reaching up, I hook her waistband while staring in her eyes. "Let me see your pretty little pussy."

She reaches down, taking my hands in hers for a moment before submitting and letting me tug her panties down. I push them down her sexy thighs and beyond her knees before they fall to the floor and she steps out of them. I fight the urge to drop to my knees to taste her, knowing that it'd be too much, too soon, but thankfully, the sweet, musky scent of her arousal envelops me and I'm drawn to seek out the source.

I slide my knee between hers, forcing her legs to spread wide and expose her pussy to the cool air of the room. She gasps, arching, and I hear the wet sound of her drenched lips spreading for me.

I let my finger skim her pussy again, from opening to clit and back around, making loops around her sensitive core but never staying exactly where she wants me. I want to drive her wild with desire, so much so that she forgets her self-imposed rules and gives in to what we both want so badly. She moans, and I remind her, hot breath in her ear, "Shh . . . quiet. We don't want people outside to hear your pleasure. That's mine . . . yours . . . *ours*."

She bites her lip, trying hard to obey. I give in too, focusing my attention on her hard clit, feeling her heartbeat pulsing as she gets higher and higher, closer to coming on my hand. "Is this where you want me? Right here on your little clit, rubbing it hard and fast to get you off like a naughty girl in my office against the door?"

"Fuck, Liam, I'm close. It's different . . .feels so good . . .had no idea . . ." She rambles and my ego swells at the mess I'm making of her. Arianna Hunnington coming undone is one of the most spectacularly beautiful sights I've ever had the pleasure to witness.

Needing to see the full breadth of her undoing, I order her, "That's it, doll. Come for me. Let that pretty virgin pussy come all over my fingers and coat me with your sweet-girl cum."

She shudders, crying out, and I cover her lips with a kiss. She's not aware enough to kiss me back, but I keep kissing her open mouth, muffling her sexy noises. I can feel the throbbing pull as her pussy clenches emptily, wanting to be filled, but I let her ride out her orgasm with my fingers still blurring on her clit, drawing as much pleasure as I can out of her body. "Oh, God," she moans, coming back to Earth.

I slow my attention to her clit, then lift my fingers to my

mouth, sucking them clean and finally getting to taste her. "Fuck, you taste like candy, doll. I want to eat you up."

She can see that I'm considering dropping to my knees to do just that, and she stops me, a bit of awkwardness taking her body. "Mr. Blackstone. Uhm . . . Liam?"

I grin. "Arianna, I think you can call me Liam, considering what we just did."

She smirks, fire returning to her eyes as the haze of lust clears. "Fair enough, sir," she says, sassing me with the name I told her to call me as we began. I nod, letting her know that works too, and her smile grows exponentially. "Liam, that was . . . wow."

"That was only the beginning, a perfect start to more." I cup her face in my hands, giving her a series of soft kisses to soften her up. "Come work for me as my secretary. Let me teach you the business side you want to know, and let me show you the wonders your body is capable of."

I see a flash in her eyes, so fast I'm not sure if I imagined it. "And what if I only want the business lessons? Only want those experiences to further my career?"

My heart stops as my eyes lock on hers, wide with shock. Really? After coming like a damn freight train on my hand, she thinks to deny that? Deny herself and me of that pleasure, all for some Prince Charming fantasy she dreamed up as a child?

I hate the thought of it and honestly don't know if I can handle being in an office every day with her without touching her, but I'm a gentleman on occasion, and this is one of the situations that requires that of me. I step back, mourning the loss of contact. "If that's what you want, Arianna."

She follows my steps, matching me and pressing her curves against mine once again as she wraps her arms around my neck. "That's not what I want, but I needed to be sure."

I look at her in confusion for a second and then her smile and words click. "It was a test? You're testing me." She looks a bit abashed but nods. "Doll, I'll let that one pass because I understand why, but do not test me again. I'll keep that in mind when we begin your *lessons* tomorrow." I let her wonder if I mean business or physical, but honestly, I plan on testing her limits for both. "You have two weeks left of your internship, during which you need to impress me enough to procure an offer of fall employment. If you were to work for me, you'd learn more at my side than your university would teach you in years, so I'd think you'd want that opportunity. I have two weeks to impress you too, enough to get between those sweet thighs and fill that untouched pussy with my cock. I know that would be an experience neither of us would ever forget, so I definitely want that honor. The two are not mutually inclusive or exclusive but exist as co-goals for us both. Understood?"

She smiles back, a full grin that lets me know the game is on. Luckily for me, I'm a damn good player and I'm not afraid to cheat if it wins me what I want . . . her. Body, mind, and soul. "Deal," she says, sealing her fate and making a deal with the devil.

"Okay, Ms. Hunnington," I say, emphasizing her name to let her know we're working in the professional realm now. "Please check in with Jacob on the way out. He can give you the appropriate contracts to sign for working at this level. I trust you can go over the contracts yourself?"

She nods. "Yes, Mr. Blackstone. Of course."

"Good. Then spend the afternoon with Jacob doing that and whatever else he needs. I'm afraid I'm out of the office this afternoon so I won't be able to hold your hand as you adjust to your new role." Every word is clipped and professional, but my cocky grin is full of mischief.

And the clock begins on what promises to be an interesting two weeks.

CHAPTER 5

ARIANNA

*ear Diary,*

WHEN I WAS TWELVE, I HAD BUTTER FOR THE FIRST TIME. Oh, sure, my mother had put plenty of yellow stuff on top of bread, mashed potatoes, all that. But it was margarine or some other substitute.

But for my twelfth birthday, Grandpa took me to a nice restaurant, and I felt so grown up. It was the summer after Grandma died, and looking back, I think he knew it would be the last big dinner he and I had together. We sat down at the table, and I remember he ordered shrimp scampi for himself and lobster for me. "But Grandpa, I hate seafood," I complained, and he shushed me, murmuring something about frozen fish sticks not being real seafood, but that was all I'd ever had.

"Arianna, you're going to change your mind with this."

When the food came . . . oh, my God, it was delicious! Even the bread tasted different, and after I mowed through the whole meal like I hadn't eaten in a week, I asked Grandpa why. He smiled, looking a little sad as he set his knife down. "Honey, sometimes, having the real thing is worth what you have to pay for it. Sometimes, it's a financial cost, like butter. Sometimes, it's something else. But you have to decide whether the reward is worth the cost."

Those words were running around my head all last night as I thought about what Liam and I did in his office. Holy fuck, was it intense. I have never experienced something so raw. And I think the reality of his fingers on my clit instead of my own or a toy was well worth the price I had to pay . . . some painful, embarrassing honesty and one appropriately-pitched temper tantrum at his abrupt jump into the deep end.

I think we both came out of that office with a better idea of who I am. And though I might've been called a whore before, I refuse to actually be one. But I am a hard worker, a fast learner, and a sure bet to use this opportunity to make the best future for myself that I can. Professionally, not on my knees.

I can't believe I'm going to be able to pick his brain for the next two weeks! I can't believe he wants to fuck me in the next two weeks either.

"HEY, SUPER NERD!" I GUSH INTO THE PHONE, NEEDING my best friend right now. Daisy Phillips is truly a nerd . . . in all the best ways, cute, with black-rimmed glasses and just a hint of shyness when she meets new people, and an intelligence for numbers most people can't begin to fathom. Drawing her as a dorm-mate and becoming friends with her is one of the best things to ever happen to me.

"Oh, my gosh, Ari! It's been forever. I've missed you!" she gushes back.

It hasn't been that long since we talked, just a week or so, but for girls who are used to seeing each other daily, it seems like ages. With a sigh, I realize we won't ever be roomies again. When I came to my internship, I took a small short-term rental for the summer to be closer to work and Daisy moved in with her boyfriend, Connor. Her boyfriend who also happens to be a math professor at the university we attend. In fact, he was her math professor. But somehow, they beat the odds, ones that Daisy or Connor could probably calculate in their heads if you wanted the real statistics, which I don't. I just care that she's happy, and she definitely seems to be that.

"How's pseudo-married life treating you?" I ask, knowing they're not married yet.

"So good! Seriously, I found out that Connor can cook, like actual food, not Ramen and canned beefaroni." She laughs, knowing that those are the quintessential college kid foods and arguably some of my comfort-food favorites, a little slice of poor-kid home life away at school. "What about you? Has your internship gotten any better?"

I take a big breath, knowing this is going to be a major chatter session. "Chica, sit down, okay? I need to brain dump a massive amount of 'what the fuck' on you because I could really use your advice, okay?"

I can hear the rustling on her end as she finds a place to curl up. "Okay, hit me."

I give her the rundown of my delivery-turned-photo-shoot, including every naughty detail of how Liam felt pressed against me, how thick and hard his cock got while the camera was clicking away, and how turned on I'd been. Luckily, she's used to hearing dirty talk like that from me so she doesn't so much as stutter until I tell her about my interview and the ensuing madness.

"Uhm, what?" she exclaims. "You're a what? Our connection must have dropped because I could've sworn you said you're a virgin, Ari." Her voice is full of confusion.

"I did, Daisy. I know, I'm sorry for not telling you, especially when you were going through all that stuff with Connor, but you always believed the façade I put on and I didn't know how to go back and straighten that out. Forgive me?" I beg, hoping she does because I don't want this to be a stumble in our friendship.

"Of course, I forgive you. It's your body, your secret, your story, but I do hope you'll tell me why the big act one day." I can hear the hurt in her voice.

"I will, I promise. But it's water under the bridge, and I need help with where I am now. Liam offered to let me complete my internship in his office, which is basically a dream come true, with a cherry topper that if I do well, he'll hire me part-time when school starts. No-brainer, right? But it's all tied up in him wanting to pop my cherry, which when I'm clear-headed and not lust-addled, sounds sketchy as fuck. But Daisy, there's something about him. I've never felt anything like this."

My brain flashes back to him crowding me against the door to finger my pussy and the way he savored my taste from his fingers. He is the Devil. And I made a deal with him. A deal for my body and my brain. Daisy interrupts my thoughts. "That sounds familiar." I can hear the smirk in her voice.

"I hear you, but this is different," I argue. Glancing at the clock, I realize I need to get ready for work or I'll be late, and that's a definite no-no. I hustle to my closet, grabbing a pencil skirt and blouse and slipping them on awkwardly as I hold the phone to my shoulder.

She laughs. "To-may-toe, to-mah-toe. Point is, you've been saving yourself for some special guy. Maybe that's the one you marry, maybe it's not. But it should be someone who makes you *feel*, someone you know will make it good, so maybe that's Liam? If so, hit that, girl. If not, that's okay. And you can still take advantage of the chance to learn as much as possible. You said he specifically said he'd still teach you, even if you didn't fuck him, right?"

I scoff. "Of course, or I'd have been out of there."

She laughs. "Exactly. You're a smart woman, so don't let him dictate your future. Choose for you . . . for both work and personal. And he can damn well play catch-up if he's not next to you every step of the way, but something tells me he's going to be right by your side or the one pulling you along."

I grin. "Damn, girl. When did you get so wise?"

"Hey, I went through a bit of hell and had to chase what I wanted and fight for it too, so I've got some advice skills. I'm just glad you're calling now instead of waiting like I did. Just be careful, honey." She's right. When Daisy finally talked to me about Connor, it'd only been because someone had forced her hand and she'd been freaking out.

"But look how well that turned out, chica. Thanks so much, truly." We say our goodbyes and hang up. I'm struck once again by what a great friend she is. But with that thought, I realize I need to hustle.

I double-check my makeup and hair, slip on my nicest pair of heels, and look in the mirror one more time. I look like a powerful woman, ready to embrace her future. Whether that's in the boardroom or the bedroom or both remains to be seen, but for now, I'm ready to roll.

WALKING INTO THE LOBBY, I PASS DORA ON MY WAY toward the elevator.

"Arianna!"

I stop, going over to be polite. "Hi, Dora. Sorry you're getting shorthanded here. Are they sending someone to help?"

Dora shakes head. "Not yet. Seriously, is this for real? I send you upstairs and the next day you're the boss's secretary?"

She looks me up and down, and I can read her thoughts

as if she spoke them aloud. She's thinking the same damn thing people always think when they only see the obvious, that I'm some ditzy floozy who gets by on her looks. They never stop to consider that maybe I succeed in spite of my looks, not because of them. I do have a brain, and I'm quite adept at using it.

"Yes, apparently so. It's a great opportunity and I'm looking forward to it," I say as politely as I can, though my inner bitch wants to snark at Dora for daring to assume she knows a damn thing about me after sending me for coffee for two months.

"Hrrmph, there is such a thing as paying your dues, Ms. Hunnington. You'd do well to know your place, especially considering you're only going to be here for such a short period of time. Just two more weeks, right?" Her voice is saccharin, as if it's a pity I'll be leaving, but I know she'd be happy if I turned and left, never to return, right now.

"Speaking of knowing my place, guess I'd better get upstairs," I reply, just as fake-sweet. And with a small wave, I head to the elevator. Kill them with kindness, I think. Play the part.

After the elevator doors close, the nerves really set in and I wonder if I'm going to get upstairs to discover this is some elaborate ruse at my expense.

Haha . . . gotcha. You didn't really think I wanted you on the top floor, did you? Stupid girl.

But I quiet the doubts and self-talk with a few slow, deep breaths, even if the other three people on the elevator look at me oddly. I don't know if it's because they're wondering who I am and why I'm going upstairs or if it's because I'm doing breathing exercises. Either way, they exit, and finally, I'm alone for the final leg of the long elevator ride.

I really don't know what to expect. While I was a receptionist, I wasn't a secretary. I think I know the basics. I mean, it's answering phones, typing stuff, probably fetching coffee . . . but something tells me that Mr. Blackstone is going to want something sweeter than sugar.

The thought thrills me and scares me all at the same time, and before I know it, the elevator doors open and I step out. Everything looks like business as usual. Everyone knows what they're doing . . . and they're going about doing it.

Yep, I think as I take a deep, nervous breath, *everyone here is a total pro . . . except you.*

I push away my momentary self-doubt and remember that I'm getting a chance to get plugged directly into the brain trust, to learn from the best, and that's like an electric charge to my spine.

After a moment, I head toward Mr. Blackstone's office and knock on the door.

I wait for a moment and then peek inside. He isn't here. Neither is Jacob.

I glance about and realize that in the external office, another small desk has been added overnight. Mr. Wilkes's desk remains in the same spot, but the line of chairs on the right side of the room has been replaced with an oak desk and cabinet. I walk over and see a note taped to the computer screen. It says Arianna on the front, and I flip it over.

In a meeting until 10:30. I expect to have these things done for me by the time I'm back.
Coffee, black.
One egg sandwich from the 2nd floor, over-easy. I have a tab.
Read the Eastern Regional Report and have a synopsis prepared.
Your pussy, nice and wet for me.

Under the last line is a cursive L with a little swirl of ink underneath, and excitement thrums through me. I shiver as I think about how his fingers felt on me, and my clit starts to throb, wanting it again. If that's what he's gonna do to me with a simple note, I'm going to have to start bringing a change of panties.

Looking over my desk, I find the report and peruse it, getting the gist of how the eastern region is doing, complete with projections and areas of growth. A quick call down to the second floor informs me that they'll happily deliver Mr. Blackstone's sandwich right at the stroke of ten thirty, so that's taken care of. After that, I search for the coffee maker, finding it hidden behind a sliding cabinet door on the minibar. I giggle a bit at that, like the coffee pot can't be out for eyes to see? I grin at the thought, though I realize it's probably more testimony to my poor upbringing than his wealthier bourgeois style. It's a bit complicated to work the thing, but after a few minutes, I have it set up and ready to go.

I stop for a moment, realizing that I've completed my to-do list, and I glance around, once again awed by the splendor of the room. It is truly stunning, and looking out at the city skyline through the floor-to-ceiling windows, my breath's taken away again.

A sudden urge comes over me and I go behind Mr. Blackstone's desk, running my hand over the plush leather of his chair. This is where I want to be. The queen of my destiny. Turning the chair to the side, I do what probably every secretary in history has done and sink down into it, feeling it envelope me as I feel the bolt of power from sitting on the throne. Wiggling back, a soft sigh escapes my lips.

"A chair fit for a king," I murmur, "or queen."

Knowing it's wrong but not able to help myself, I kick my legs up on his desk, just for a second, and my mind wanders to a future where this is my reality. Yep, this is the life for me.

I must lose track of time for a moment because I'm surprised when the door springs open. I jump to my feet as Liam walks in, every bit the powerful CEO. He's wearing navy blue today, not gray, but other than that, he's just as sexy as yesterday, and my heart thumps in my chest as I take him in.

He pauses, his eyes roving over me. The hair on my forearms stands up as I blush, knowing I'm busted. "Mr. Blackstone."

"Getting comfortable, I see," he says with an arrogant smirk. Behind him, I can see Mr. Wilkes, looking not too pleased.

"I . . . umm," I stammer before hanging my head. "I'm sorry."

He chuckles as he walks toward the windows. He gestures to the space next to him, and I obediently stand beside him, following his gaze over the city below as I brush a lock of hair behind my ear. "You don't have to explain or apologize. You said this is your dream, so you're checking things out. It's enticing, no?"

He leans over, and I'm enveloped by the cologne that I love. Sweet leather. I have to learn what the hell the name of that stuff is because partnered with his natural scent, it's like an aphrodisiac straight to my core.

"It was my dream once, too, and I made it my reality," he says, but he's not looking at his office or the view. He's looking at me.

I gulp, and he glances behind us. There's a soft click, and I realize that Jacob has left and we're alone once again. Liam moves to his chair, sitting down comfortably, the crown invisible but no less present with the power emanating from him. "Did you complete your list, Arianna?"

He glances down my body pointedly, but I'm not that easy. I remember Daisy's advice to be strong and see if he stays with me. "I did, Mr. Blackstone," I say, purposefully using the name to differentiate what mode we're currently in. "Breakfast will be delivered in minutes. Would you like your coffee now?"

He dips his chin, an amused smirk on his face, like he knows what I'm doing and is getting a kick out my attempt to act unaffected by him. I'm sure he can see the flush on my face, but I press on, grabbing a mug and filling it with the dark brew. The aroma fills my senses, lessening the effect of his cologne and waking me up even without the caffeine dose. I set the coffee down in front of him, but instead of drinking it, he asks, "And the Eastern Region report?"

"Yes, sir. It's in your inbox." I pick up the file from the corner of his desk. "Would you like the synopsis?"

He gestures widely with his hands, giving me the floor. I come around to his side, placing the folder in front of him and turning to the report so he can follow along as I speak. "Second-quarter figures were trending up, and that was expected to continue. However, third-quarter shows stabilizing numbers."

He interrupts me. "Why did you look at the second quarter if I told you I wanted a synopsis of the third-quarter report?"

I glance at him in surprise. "Because without the relevant framework, the figures are useless. They're only helpful in the scheme of up, down, or staying the same. Knowing that we had $55 million in sales could be cause for celebration or to close the doors, but that's only knowable in context." He inclines his head, and I think I might've jumped a notch in his estimation. "As I was saying, the stabilizing figures indicate . . ." and I continue a brief summarization.

I'm standing over him as he sits, a power position, but it's a false show because we both know who the boss is in this room. And though he's nodding along as I give my report, he's distracting me, letting his fingertips trace along my arm and up my thigh. "Please focus, Arianna. Being focused is the only way to succeed, and you do want to succeed, don't you?" He smirks at me. The cocky bastard knows what he's doing to me.

Suddenly, he snaps, "Enough. Excellent summarization. Now, about the rest of the list . . ." He closes the file, setting it aside and pulling me between his spread legs, my ass resting along the edge of the desk.

I knew he silently promised this, but there's no way we could do this every day and actually get work done. And while the idea of seeing what Mr. Blackstone has to offer, I'm here for more than that. I have a goal, and getting lost in how badly I want him isn't helping me accomplish that.

Liam, though, seems to be unconcerned. "Did you complete your final task? Is this pussy wet and ready for me?"

I bite my lip, hedging my answer. "I am . . . wet, but I don't know about ready."

The smug tilt of his lips says he thinks otherwise. "Have you ever heard of edging?"

"No," I rasp, my head spinning as he cups my breast through my blouse, his fingers tugging on my stiffening nipple through my thin bra. "What's—"

Before I can finish, he lifts me onto the desk, his hands slipping up my skirt along my inner thighs to palm my pussy through my damp panties.

"Edging," he whispers huskily in my ear, sounding almost like a teacher or instructor, "is when I get you so close to the edge, but right before you fall off, I let up. Then, when you calm down a little, I do it again . . . and again . . . and again. It's sweet, sweet torture, but oh, so delectable."

"Oh, God," I moan as his hand massages my pussy, rolling his fingers between my lips, soaking the fabric of my panties. "What in the hell are you doing?"

"Lift up," he hisses, and when I do, he slides my panties down my thighs, tucking them into his desk drawer with an evil grin. I wonder what he's going to do with them later, but the thought flies out of my head when he starts tweaking my clit. "I'm teaching you, Babydoll. I'm showing you that patience is essential, along with control and the ability to hold steady, even when your body screams for something else. Like last night. Do you think I went home and jacked off as I thought about how you will look with that 'O' on your face as my cock slides inside you?"

I moan, his powerful fingers doing amazing things to me as he talks dirty to me. "Oh, fuck. Did you?"

His massage of my core is so good that I'm almost ready to come, but he pulls back, chuckling. "No," he whispers. "I didn't. Just like you aren't . . . until I'm ready to *let* you."

His words hit me hard, and I whimper, looking at him. "Please," I moan, my body quivering. "I need—"

"Please, what?" Liam asks, lifting an eyebrow, his fingers still touching me but not moving at all.

"Please, sir, let me come."

He starts again, bringing me to the brink with his fingers on my clit and teasing along my entrance. I desperately need more, his finger inside me or for him to stay focused on my clit, but he stops again. It's like he said, sweet torture as my pussy feels swollen, puffy, and aching, my fingers gripping the edge of his desk so hard I've got cramps threatening in my forearms. But I can only think of one thing.

"Please," I beg again.

He bends closer, eyes locked onto my pussy, and though I know I should tell him to stop, I can't. He's increasing the price, but when his tongue swipes across my aching clit, it's an expense I'll gladly pay. "Oh, God," I cry out, trying so hard to be quiet.

The feel of his tongue on my pussy is more than I could have ever imagined. Hot, wet, and a completely different sensation from his fingers. And when he moans against my sensitive skin, the vibration nearly sends me over.

"Fuck, doll. You taste like candy, so sweet I want to drink you down." I think that's exactly what he's doing as he covers my pussy with his mouth, sucking my sensitive skin and flicking his tongue across my engorged clit.

I can feel my body building up to something massive, something I've never experienced before. If this is edging, I want to do it all the time. I suspect it has more to do with the man between my thighs than some trick of orgasm denial though.

He pulls me tighter against his face, my pussy chasing his tongue unashamedly. "You want to come?" he says. I nod, whimpering. "What are you willing to give for it?" he asks, stroking a finger once over my lips. I cry out. I'm closer than ever, but he knows just what he's doing.

My mouth drops open, then I shut it with a snap as I glare at him, the denial starting to fray the edges of my patience. There's no way I'm going to give up this easily, this quickly, but I'll be damned if he doesn't tempt me. I open my mouth again, looking down at him. "Loyalty."

"I don't want your loyalty." He snickers. "I'll earn that in time. No . . . I want your obedience."

I gulp, knowing I'm handing him some of the power that he promised me yesterday . . . but not too much. "But what do you want me to do?"

Liam grins. "Stay still and let me fuck you with my tongue. Don't make a sound."

I nod, gritting my teeth as he massages me, spreading my lips wide open to his gaze. It's so hard not to cry out, my chest aching and my fingers knotting as I grip the desk tightly. He slips the tip of his tongue into my pussy, just barely penetrating me, but it's so much better. It's a hint of what I really want, what I need, but he's still teasing me, barely thrusting inside as he lazily rubs his thumb across my clit.

I can feel the fire building in my stomach, and I'm about to explode when there's a knock at the door. "Mr. Blackstone? There's something that needs your attention."

"Fuck," Liam hisses, his mouth and fingers deserting me.

He pushes his chair back and adjusts his pants, pulling

me from the desk and handing me the folder he'd set aside. "Sit in the chair, doll."

"What?" I ask, shocked. "Are you—"

My body obeys while my mind catches up, and as I walk from between his legs, he swats my ass with a soft smack. I look back sharply, and he grins, making sure I see him wiping my juices from his mouth and sucking his fingers clean.

I've barely set my ass in his chair when he yells out, "Come in."

CHAPTER 6

LIAM

I'm hard as a rock and glad my desk covers me as Jacob and Melvin Jackson walk in the door. Jacob leads the way, looking around like he's probably guessed what was going on with Arianna, but he doesn't know for sure, and I'm going to keep it that way as long as I can to save myself from the lecture. Melvin is a lanky, odd-looking fellow who could double as Norman Bates with glasses, and he always comes off as nervous for some reason. He was already working at Morgan when I took over and has been helpful during the transition to my leadership. Not sure exactly how he got that gig because technically, he doesn't even work on this floor, but he showed up one day with some interesting figures and some intel to share, so he's been useful, at least.

"Yes?" I ask, tilting my head. "You did say it was important?"

Melvin looks to Jacob, who nods. Jacob intends the nod to give Melvin permission to speak, but Melvin reads it incorrectly and takes it as the go-ahead to sit in my guest chair. The one right next to Arianna.

He looks over at her, and I notice his eyes stay strictly on her face, not scanning her lush curves. He might've just gone up a small notch in my estimation because if he'd looked at her body, I would've been tempted to teach him a lesson about looking at what's mine.

Wait . . . what? She's not mine, and I'm not some Neanderthal. But the urge to mark her, claim her, sits in my gut like a stone. It might not be politically correct, and I suspect she'd kick me in the balls if I verbalized my thoughts aloud, but it's the possessive impulse I feel. I wonder if Jacob and Melvin can smell the sweetness of her sex in the air of my office or if they realize why Arianna's cheeks are flushed? I waver between pride, knowing that she's only that undone because of me, and fury, greedy that only I see her that way.

Melvin reaches out a hand to Arianna, "Melvin Jackson, Vice President of Business Analytics." She takes his hand for a quick shake, introducing herself too.

And then Melvin turns his attention to me. Finally. "Sir, I just wanted to say that I think you've done a great job since taking over as CEO this summer. The figures show a significant uptick in public perception and stock indexes are expected to reflect that."

"Appreciated, but if that's all, Melvin, I'm really—"

"But there are whispers," Melvin says quickly. He glances back at Arianna, obviously uncertain whether he should say what he wants to in front of her.

I glance to Jacob, who nods. Apparently, I need to hear whatever Melvin is dishing. "It's okay, Melvin. You can speak freely in front of Arianna." My words elicit similar reactions in them both, eyes widening and eyebrows raising. Arianna quickly schools her features, though I can read her delight at getting some insight on the inner workings of Morgan. Melvin still looks unsure, but he continues.

"Sir, when you took over, you brought with you a . . . well, some people are calling it a 'rockstar' attitude. You have to understand, Morgan has always had a more traditional corporate culture. We've succeeded for years on a solid business model of predicting the market and being there before the competitors. But the changes you are implementing? There is concern that perhaps you're more flash than substance. That perhaps you simply don't understand what has made Morgan the company it is today, what we stand for, or who we are."

"They brought me in to shake things up, and my track record speaks for itself," I reply. "Melvin, this company lost millions last year and needs a fast turnaround to stay at the forefront of the market you're trying to predict. I don't want Morgan to follow along like sheep, chasing dollars and market shares. I want to create the market trends, have the other companies scrambling to catch up with us. Just give it some time and you'll see. My way works."

He nods but is still unsatisfied. "But sir, I think you'll see in our third-quarter reports that sales are at respectable levels, and moving into the fourth quarter, I predict we'll see similar numbers, maybe even an increase of one to two percent, which could be extremely beneficial for Morgan's bottom line."

I sigh. "Third-quarter reports? I was just going over the Eastern Region report this morning," I say, giving Arianna a quick glance. "While the numbers look good, if you compare them with the second quarter, you can see that they're trending down." Arianna uncrosses and recrosses her legs, drawing my attention. I offer her a smile, acknowledging that I'm repeating her synopsis from this morning. But I didn't need her to tell me that. I already knew. I'd just wondered if she'd take initiative and what her summary of the report would show . . . a regurgitation of the numbers or a more thoughtful analysis? Luckily, my smart girl knows her stuff and dug deeper.

"And beyond the quarter to quarter changes, look back to last year's third quarter. We're down almost nine percent since then. Unacceptable, especially considering we had a product availability increase in the area. Status-quo thinking doesn't get status-quo results. If we stay stagnant and don't change our MO, Morgan will fail, and I refuse to let that happen. So, innovative thinking and new possibilities are the direction we're heading."

Melvin bows his head for a moment, frustration written in the lift of his shoulders, which are nearing his ears. He sighs. "Very well, sir. If you're certain that is the best path, perhaps you should amp up the 'rockstar' a bit for the board then. Really sell them on your plan, explain your business model of change, and that they should believe in your ideas. Get them on board in a big way so that we can be a team again."

It's not a bad idea. But I'm not used to explaining myself. I usually do my analysis with Jacob and we get to work, creating success where none existed before. But he might have a point in this particular case since the board and many of the executives are rather old-school, Melvin included. They'd definitely prefer more intel. I'm just not certain whether I want to give it to them. "I'll take that under advisement, Melvin. If there's nothing else?" It's an obvious dismissal, and he gets up, nodding at me, then Arianna. He basically ignores Jacob as he walks to the door and strides out.

Jacob looks at me, nonplussed. "You could've handled that better." He plops down into the chair Melvin just vacated. He doesn't need an invite or permission since he's my best friend and my right-hand guy at the office.

I shake my head. "It's the truth. Do you believe that guy?"

"You didn't really give him a chance to speak. Some of the stuff he told me . . ." Jacob says after a moment. "I don't know. Like, some of the executives are uncomfortable with your new direction and chatting among themselves. I think one comment he says he heard was 'this isn't the eighties, and he isn't Gordon fucking Gekko.' He said he might've even overheard the word 'takeover' from one, but he wasn't sure who it was. Hallway chatter, apparently."

"No one has given me that impression. I've gotten nothing but praise from the board," I muse. "And they asked me here, knowing Morgan needed some drastic action to stay solvent." It's times like this that I appreciate Jacob. He's my sounding board and trusted advisor. "What do you think? Should I be worried?"

Jacob scratches at the stubble on his jaw. "I don't know. I haven't heard anything that's bad, but Melvin is part of a certain inner circle. They might be whispering behind closed doors. I could see the comment being made by some people."

"Fuck them. They're comparing me to a fictional asshole," I growl, hating the comparison. "Why bring me in to begin with if they want me to conform to the same old thinking? All the hoopla that surrounds me is just the window dressing. It's called creating buzz. We've done this before, us against the old regime. We're good and what we do works."

Jacob shrugs, unconcerned. "You're good, Liam. But you have rocked some boats." He glances at Arianna and then back to me. I eye him, letting him know in our nonverbal shorthand to watch his step because I can see where this is going.

"Pulling up Arianna to be your secretary probably didn't help matters. It's raised some eyebrows. And I'm not going to ask what you two have been doing for the past thirty minutes."

Arianna shrinks in her chair, her cheeks blushing furiously. If there was any doubt, she might as well have shouted from the rooftop what we've been up to. Jacob is broaching on some treacherous waters, and I warn him off so he doesn't piss me off too badly. I snap, "Jacob, watch it."

"Look, whatever you two do outside the office is none of my business. On your own time, that's all well and good. But here? We need to stay on task. We're mid-transition and implementing big changes that make folks uncomfortable. Adding in some crazy 'rockstar' shit like fucking an intern in your office" —he turns to Arianna— "or fucking the CEO, is dangerous." Arianna gasps, horrified and embarrassed at his words.

I growl, ready to tear into Jacob, but he holds up a staying hand, and only because of years of friendship do I let him speak. "HR has already been hounding me about why a new job was created without their procedures being followed. You can hire and fire assistants at will, but the way you did it? It's just another tally in the 'doesn't follow the rules' column."

"Okay, Jacob, you've said your piece and you're done. It's my turn. You're just doing your job, and I get that, but there are going to be pissed-off people. There always are when we come in and start changing shit. And you're right, what I do outside the office, or inside," I snarl, "is none of your business. But a secretary is a good thing for us both. Arianna can help me, but she can also help you. Feel free to offload some of your duties to her so that we can work on the higher-level stuff for the board. She can do more than make copies and coffee, so use her. I want her to learn."

Jacob and I have a war with our eyes, neither of us willing to give in to the other. Finally, he sighs and turns to Arianna. "I've read your file. I know you're smart . . .

3.85 GPA in international business with a minor in finance, and impressive internships and references. But one of my jobs is to protect Liam. Do I need to protect him from you?"

It's a blunt question, and not one I foresaw him asking. Arianna seems to take it stride, having recovered enough from her initial mortification at being called out to watch my exchange with Jacob closely, though I can still see the slight flush to her cheeks. "Mr. Wilkes, working for Morgan has been a dream of mine. Professionally, getting to be a fly on the wall and watch Mr. Blackstone work at turning this ship around is an experience I wouldn't dare mess up. Personally, while it is a delicate dance, we are figuring things out appropriately, and rest assured it will not affect my professionalism nor have ugly ramifications in the future."

Usually, when people couch what they're saying in business lingo, I tune out the droning. But listening to Arianna slay business babble is apparently a new turn-on for me, especially when she says we're figuring things out. Because I'm damn sure figuring her out, bit by bit, response by response, and I like what I'm learning about her.

Jacob looks between the two of us and sighs again, rolling his eyes, but he seems to be a little less concerned. "Okay. I hear you. I'm with you all the way, no matter what. Just saying, a little tact goes a long way."

"Yeah, well, so does a little recognition. You know I'm not going to let my personal life interfere with what we're doing. We're already turning this company around, Jacob. You and me. We've busted our asses, given up a shitload of nights out, and had too many cold dinners at home to count. Now we're here, and nothing's going to stop us. This isn't a one-man show, no matter what the image might be."

Jacob nods. "Thanks for that, Liam. I'll do my best, then. I won't let you down."

"That's the spirit. Now, look at my desk. See the coffee and my sandwich? That's two duties you don't have to do from now on."

Jacob looks at the sandwich and then to Arianna before laughing a little. "Great, my two easiest duties taken care of. Now what will I do with all my spare time?"

"Keep my ass out of the fire," I reply, shifting a little. Despite my bravado, Melvin's comments could be a problem. "If I'm causing a divide within the company this early in the game, we'll do well to listen to the rumblings . . . just a little bit."

Jacob nods and stands, leaving the weight of his concerns on my shoulders. But he gives both me and Arianna a pointed look as he closes the door. He's watching us, making sure we don't misstep or let this, whatever this is, affect work. It's not what I typically ask of him, but I'm damn sure he's got my back. And maybe Arianna's too.

She looks back to me, and I can see the wheels turning in her mind as she processes everything she just witnessed, evaluating it for every nugget of information she can glean. Finally, she says, "Now what?"

When most people ask me a question like that, it's

because they're waiting for me to set the course and to proceed, ready to follow me to the slaughterhouse if I deem it, like sheeple following their leader. Me. But when Arianna asks that, it almost feels like she's already decided on the proper course of action and she's testing me to see if I have the right answer. The thought that she might consider that she knows more than I do amuses me, but at the same time, I respect her mind and am curious what she has in hers. "You tell me."

She dips her chin in deference, recognizing the gift of power I just bestowed on her. "We need to be discreet and careful. Neither of us wants our professional career marred with some office romance scandal. I'm here to learn, and you can teach me so much. I don't want to lose that opportunity. Nor can you allow your apparently tenuous hold on the board to be muddied by it coming out that you're fucking your intern."

I grin. She's not wrong. But I didn't get to where I am now, sitting in this leather chair at the head of an international business empire, by playing it safe. Risk is inherent. Risk is what begets reward. When calculated correctly, risk is the stepping stone that jumps you ahead of all safe moves. "You're right. But I'm not fucking my intern . . . yet," I say, using her sexy crude language right back at her. "And I do have so much to teach you, Ms. Hunnington. For example . . . come here."

"What?" she sputters, unsure at the game I'm playing because my plan is so counterintuitive to her own well-thought-out, responsible choice.

"Come. Here. Arianna." I let the authority I have over

her, both professional and intimate, filter into the words, giving them a heavy weight of command. She rises, slowly but surely walking to my side. I lean back in my chair for a moment, head tilted as I scan her up and down, intentionally pausing on the curves of her ass and tits. I can see her chest rising as her breathing gets faster. Without warning, I grab her hips, yanking her between my legs once again and pushing her back on my desk, just like she was before we were interrupted. Her gasp of surprise is like a shot of adrenaline through my veins. Her hands on my shoulders as she works to steady herself from the fast movement is the only thing holding me to earth.

"Lift." She puts her palms on the desk, lifting her hips so I can slide her skirt back up to her waist. Her bare pussy is still wet for me, maybe even wetter, I realize, as I see the wetness spreading along her thighs from where she's crossed her legs.

"I agree we need to be on our best behavior over the next couple of days while I smooth some ruffled feathers."

She looks down at me, the fire back in her eyes. "You don't strike me as a man who lets people tell him what to do."

"I don't," I reply, spreading her legs and pulling her to the edge of the desk so that she's right in front of my hungry eyes. "I do what I want. I'm just taking a few precautions. The long game. And even I know when some rules should be followed."

She gasps as I grab handfuls of her lush thighs, pulling

her pussy wide open so I can see every inch of her pinkness. "Doesn't that mean—"

"And when some rules can be bent or broken. Don't worry, doll, I still intend on giving you more than you can handle," I continue, bending down to lick the seam where her leg joins her center. "I want a buildup . . . because I have something special planned."

She practically melts for me, her ass grinding against the desk as she nears her edge again . . . but I have no intention of letting her come. Not yet. If I'm waiting, she can damn sure wait, following me into lust-induced madness too. "What's that? Oh, God, this feels good."

"This weekend," I whisper, teasing her clit with featherlight flicks I know will torture her but not make her come, "you will stay at my place . . . and I'm going to give you what you want. You'll like that, won't you? Coming to my place . . . to learn what coming really means. Like you want to now."

My clever girl fights back, though, chasing my tongue, and I'm so very tempted to give in and let her come all over my mouth. But then she speaks around her moans. "I don't think . . . I shouldn't."

Fuck, this woman. I'm damn-near out of my mind, and she's riding my face like it's heaven she's never imagined, but she still holds back from me, still has her faculties to doubt this. I promised her I'd impress her enough to earn the space between her thighs, but I didn't know I'd have to work this fucking hard for it. I'm verging on saying fuck it and just giving in so she comes all over my mouth, but I hold back, knowing that my initial idea of teasing her until she crosses the line where need rules her body is still my best course of action.

I lay a sucking kiss on her clit, and her thighs clamp around my head, trying to keep me there. But I press her legs open with my elbows, spreading her pussy with my hands. She's right there on the edge. I know one touch will send her over. I look up at her, waiting for her eyes to snap to mine in impatience. "This weekend . . . we'll see."

And with that, I lay one last chaste kiss to her bare mound, avoiding her clit where she desperately wants me, and then sit back in my chair. Never breaking eye contact, I wipe her juices from my lips, slipping a finger into my mouth to taste her once more. She huffs, confused for a second, and I see the moment her orgasm falls away, the lust clears, and she glares at me. It might be one of the sexiest things I've ever seen.

She shoves me out of the way, jumping from the desk and shoving her skirt down. "Mother fucker. Ugh, I can't believe you." She keeps murmuring, and I hear my name a few times as she gets closer to the door.

Right as she reaches for the doorknob, I call out. "Arianna." She stops, barely turning her head to look at me. "Negotiation lesson. Everyone comes to the table with something of value, some more valuable, some less. But everyone has something. You have what I want . . . that hot, virgin pussy that I know will feel so sweet coming on my cock. I have what you want."

I pause and her eyes spark. If looks could kill, I'd be a dead man. "Not that, Arianna. I've already told you I know you're no whore. I won't be trading business for pleasure. What I bring to the table . . . is me. My desire to fuck you, show you what your body can handle, teach you about all the wonders the flesh can offer." Even I know there's more to it than that, but physical pleasure is all I can promise right now, and I hope it's enough.

"I do want that," she says, but the confession isn't the soft admission I'd expect it to be. "But I want that with one man, *The One*. Nothing more and nothing less. And though you tempt me . . ." She rolls her eyes. "Fuck, do you tempt me. I know the value of what I bring to the table, Mr. Blackstone. Sometimes, the real thing is worth the price you have to pay." She says the words like she's quoting something or someone, like she found a hidden well of strength deep within her to resist my charms.

But as she leaves, defiantly looking at me with a glare I'm sure she thinks is frosty, I can see the heat, the desire burning hot inside her. I've already got her. She just doesn't know it yet.

CHAPTER 7

ARIANNA

*D**ear Diary,*

It's been insanely hard behaving over the past few days. Every day, Liam looks at me like a starving wolf, ready to devour my body. Though I tried to stick with the cold shoulder, he quickly wore me down. I'm such a sucker, but the way his eyes track me is heady, making me feel simultaneously at his mercy and powerful, and when I get close enough, he brushes against me, subtle touches that make me burn at the contact.

Every word carries sexual undertones, and I have to admit to trying to give as good as I'm getting. I tempt him, whether to look down my blouse or to see that I'm wearing a thong. I know it makes his dick hard and hungry, and I can't help but leave these encounters with a smile, feeling victorious even though I'm playing with fire.

The power dynamic between us is constantly changing. One second, I'm teasing him, feeling every bit the vixen I'm really not, and the next, he's got me shoved up against the window as he demands 'just a taste'. And even though he hasn't let me come since that first day,

I obey every time, futilely hoping he'll let me come this time but enjoying the way he tortures me regardless.

The only thing not making me lose my mind is that he's letting me use mine, staying true to his promise to teach me. We've discussed his business evaluation of Morgan, past, present, and future. We've talked about negotiation tactics and management techniques, and I've been lucky enough to sit in on several meetings to take notes, though Jacob is always there too since he's Liam's right-hand man and has a rather amazing business mind of his own. The three of us even went to lunch yesterday, and just listening to them talk about their experiences was better than any college lecture I've ever had.

It's all been this tightrope walk of balance, professional and personal, intimate and formal, business and pleasure. And while I know I've impressed Liam a few times with my thoughts as he's questioned me, I'll admit that he's impressed me too.

But is that enough? Enough to give in on a rule I made for myself? Even if it wasn't for some big moral, ethical stance, but rather a fear-induced boundary to keep my heart safe from further hurt. But giving in might lead to exactly that, a much deeper pain than I've ever felt before. The folks back home who said shit, I didn't really care about them one way or the other.

But Liam? I am starting to care, especially as I get to know him better and see the good inside him that he dresses up in the cocky asshole business façade. It's a good front and gets the job done, because it's not like a ball-busting CEO can be a nice guy who politely asks for things. But the real Liam is a good guy just trying to make a difference and succeed.

Late one night, when it was just the two of us in the office, he even told me the story of how his dad didn't want him taking over the family business. He'd said that the critical words gave him the push to fight harder, work longer, and be stronger, but I could see the cutting pain his dad's careless words had caused.

That Liam, vulnerable and sweet, mixed with the business one, cold and calculating, and topped with his heavy-handedness with me, dominant and sexy, is doing a weird number on my mind, my body, my heart. And I'm actually considering going to his place this weekend.

Grabbing a stack of papers out of the 'work' box Jacob set up for me, I see they need to be copied and collated for the board meeting on Monday. It's busy work that'll at least keep me occupied. Anything is better than the quiet humming office white noise.

Just as I round the corner to the copy room, I run into someone, startling me so much I drop my stack of papers. "Oh!"

"Sorry about that," the guy says, bending down to pick up my papers before I can move. Thankfully, the stack was double-binder-clipped together so it's not a scattered mess.

"Me too . . . sorry. And thank you," I say as he stands back upright and hands the papers to me. I realize I know this guy. Though he's not particularly attractive, his black slightly dorky glasses are memorable. "Uhm, Melvin, right? I mean, Mr. Jackson." Shit. I totally just collided with the VP who's helping Liam.

He smiles. "You remembered?" He seems genuinely surprised. "Call me Melvin, please. Arianna, right?"

I nod. Usually, I'd be thrilled that a VP remembered my name, but though his eyes are solidly on mine and completely appropriate, there's something a little off about the guy. Like he's not checking me out, thank God, but he's analyzing me somehow. Though I remember now that he is a number cruncher, so maybe that's just how he is?

"Did I hurt you?" he asks, finally giving me a cursory head-to-toe glance.

"No, not at all. Just surprised me. Sorry again."

Feeling like the accidental interaction has reached a reasonable end and sure that Melvin has better things to do than chat with an intern, I turn to the copier and begin placing the stack of papers into the feed tray.

"Oh, I can show you a little trick for that," he says, coming over to my side. He doesn't wait for me to move, just reaches in front of me and starts pushing buttons on the big copy machine.

"I've got it. Thanks, though. I'm sure you have stuff to do." I try to argue politely.

"I insist. This will save you tons of time. See?" He taps on the screen, where the expected job completion time is now four minutes instead of the nine it had been when I'd set up the job differently.

I smile politely. "Thanks."

And cue . . . silence. Awkward silence.

Finally, he breaks the quiet. "So, are you enjoying your work for Liam?"

It strikes me as odd that he calls him Liam since he was all 'Mr. Blackstone' when they met before, but I guess I switch in and out of the casual name usage as well. Come to think of it, so does Jacob. So maybe that's just the norm around here.

"I am. I've spent the majority of my summer internship manning the front desk, which was great. But I'm definitely learning more with Mr. Blackstone and Mr. Wilkes." It's a great rah-rah, nothing critical answer, but still truthful.

Melvin smiles, but his eyes narrow. It's an odd expression, like he can't decide what the proper response should be. "I'm sure. But I do feel I should warn you . . ." He pauses, looking over his shoulder at the empty doorway. "Be careful, Arianna. Liam has a huge ego and a tendency to be an asshole." He flinches, like the word was hard for him to say, and I get the feeling he doesn't curse much. That's kind of refreshing these days when folks drop F-bombs like nothing, myself included in that group. "He's not particularly well-liked around here, so while you may be learning from him, you're at a disadvantage because not many people will want to work with you after knowing that Liam provided your business education. I'm sure you're hoping to get hired on in the fall—interns always are—but don't get too close or your image will be tied up with his and that could be disastrous."

I'm shocked, first that Melvin is telling me this stuff. I know he's supposed to be Liam's top-secret information mole or whatever, but sharing all that with some intern seems rather loose-lipped if I'm honest. Plus, it feels vaguely threatening, like I won't get hired on because I work with Liam, but I figured working for the CEO would help make me a shoe-in for a fall position. I'm not sure how to respond, so I hedge. "Thanks for the advice, Mr. Jackson. That's definitely something to keep in mind."

He blinks three times in rapid succession, his face blank. "Do remember and be careful, Arianna. I'd hate to see a young professional get side-tracked. I could put in a good word for you. I usually have a fall part-time staffer in my office to help with end-of-year report preparation. You'd like that. We should get coffee and discuss it."

Working with Melvin sounds like the ninth ring of hell, awkward and boring, but I try to be polite. "Thanks so much, Mr. Jackson. I'm really busy for Mr. Blackstone right now, but I'll talk to Mr. Wilkes about my fall place-ment." I have no intention of doing so unless it's to beg Jacob to not place me in the Business Analysis department.

"Melvin, please," he says, catching on that I've been calling him Mr. Jackson to distance myself a bit.

Thankfully, there's a commotion in the hallway, and I see Liam and Jacob walk by, lost in conversation as several other people in suits follow behind them. The copy machine beeps, and I think *saved by the bell* to myself. I grab the stack of printouts and turn. "Thanks so much, Melvin," I say, emphasizing his name, which makes him smile wanly. "But I'd better get back to the office and see if Mr. Blackstone or Mr. Wilkes needs anything."

"Of course," he says, stepping away, and I realize just how close he was. "Remember to be careful. Coffee next week?" he calls out, but I'm already out the door and down the hallway.

I hustle down the hall, catching up to Liam and Jacob. Jacob veers to his desk, and I follow Liam into his office, biting my lip as I watch his tight, firm ass flex in his pants. His suit today is especially slim-fitting, probably Italian, and making him look like a GQ model. I swear he gets better-looking each day that passes.

I don't bother telling him about the encounter with Melvin. I don't want to get involved in office politics. Besides, Liam seems rather exasperated post-meeting, much different from the usual cockily assured self he was this morning.

"How'd the meeting go?" I ask as Liam pours himself a soda water. "Anything interesting that you can tell me?"

He shakes his head, draining his glass in a swallow. "The usual. Someone proposes an idea, and the board squabbles over it, trying to pick it apart. Problem is, most of their ideas would've been great twenty years ago. Now, not so much."

"So, what happens in the end?" I ask, and Liam chuckles, setting his glass down and walking toward his desk. He drops into his leather chair, looking like the frustrated king of a wayward country.

"Either they get with the times or I come up with the

solution myself. It was a waste of precious time as they argued the pros and cons of useless ideas." I walk over to his desk, retracing his footsteps, but instead of the chair, I perch on the desk next to him.

"Tell me about the ideas. Maybe it'll help to go through them methodically to see if there's anything salvageable. Maybe you can combine a sprinkle of this and dash of that and create something the board will appreciate but still gets you the result you're looking for."

He nods and begins talking through the various proposals that were presented at the meeting. Usually, I'd be tuned in closely, absorbing every word and learning. But right now, I'm distracted. I'm enveloped by the masculine scent of his aftershave as he gestures with his hands. I watch as he scrubs a hand along the scruff on his jawline before threading his hands through his hair, mussing it, but somehow, it only looks sexier when it's slightly rough.

The frustration is palpable in his words, and as he gets to the end of his rant, I cross my legs. His eyes snap to my thighs. "I could think of a million other things I'd rather be doing than rehashing that meeting." He skims a finger along my thigh, the skirt not hiding the heat of his touch. "Or *whom* I'd rather be doing."

The fact that he shares with me, wants my opinion, wants *me*, makes me feel so powerful. Turning to him, I do something I haven't done before, take control. I don't give myself time to have second thoughts or doubts about the intelligence of my actions. I just go with it, wanting to follow my own desires and see where that leads. I rise, moving to stand between his spread legs, and place my hands on the armrests of his chair to bend forward, invading his space. "You seem stressed. Maybe I could help you relax?"

This is the first time I've taken initiative like this. I may tease and flirt, but it's always Liam who moves us into this territory. But his eyes light up instantly, seeming to like me taking the lead for a change. "What did you have in mind, doll?"

My usual mouthiness deserts me, so instead of answering, I simply drop to my knees before him. I look up through my lashes, not shy in the least, but seeking permission while refusing to ask. "You want to suck my cock? You think that'll relax me?" That arrogant smirk is in his tone, though his lips don't tilt. He cups my cheek, and I lean into the caress, my eyes slipping closed as my mouth drops open. He traces along my bottom lip, dipping his thumb into my mouth, and I instinctively close around it, sucking and licking at the pad. "Fuck, Arianna. Do it. Suck me."

My eyes pop open, and I reach forward to undo his brown leather belt, then his slacks. He yanks his shirt up to get it out of my way, and I have a moment of pause before I pull him out of his boxer briefs. I've felt him rubbing against my ass and grinding against my pussy as he's teased me all week, so I know he's big, thick, and hard. But this will be the first time I actually see his cock, and I'm excited at the anticipation of finally laying eyes on him. I pull the waistband of his boxer briefs down, and his cock surges out, rock-hard and throbbing. I take a moment, teasing a fingertip along the velvety skin as I learn him. "Fuck, Liam. You're gorgeous."

"I taste even better," he groans. I look up, and his eyes are pained, desperately needy. Glancing back down, I see a dribble of pre-cum running from the red head down his shaft.

I realize with a start, "Have you been holding off like you said? Edging me all week and not taking any relief for yourself?" He reaches down and squeezes the base of his shaft and I know my answer. "I'm impressed, Mr. Blackstone," I tease.

"I am rather impressive," he says, his voice gravelly and the bragging sounding more habitual than real.

"We'll see," I say as I lean forward, letting my pink tongue stick out to lick along his length. I get my first taste of him, musky and sweet and delicious, making me want more. His hands grip the armrests so hard his knuckles are going white. So I lick up and down, catching every bit of pre-cum before sucking along his head to get more. His hips buck slightly, so I press against him, not remotely able to hold him, but he relents and sits still for my exploration.

"Fuck, Ari . . . do that . . . suck the head again." His hands move into my hair, and I let him guide me for a moment but realize that this is my moment. I'm doing this to him, and I want that power surge, that ability to drive him as wild as he's been driving me all week. Though I plan on being kinder and actually letting him come. Maybe.

The thought of edging him, evilly getting him to the brink and then pulling back like he's done to me all week, is a wicked temptation. But when I get another mouthful of his sweet pre-cum, I know I don't have the discipline he does. I want all of him.

"Put your hands back on the armrests. Let me do this. Let me learn you, what you like," I whisper.

He lifts his head from the back of the chair, eyeing me, and I consider that he's likely never given up any shred of control like this, always the predator, the dominant, the alpha. But for me, he does as I say, laying his hands back on the armrests and letting me lead.

I feel like a boss. Like The Boss, able to bring this powerful beast of a man to his knees figuratively by being on my knees literally. And like a boss, I get to work, licking and sucking him into my mouth, sometimes just the head like he asked, but slowly learning how deep I can take him. Oh, so slowly, I get better, judging by the increasingly louder grunts and groans Liam is trying to keep quiet. He hits my throat, and I gag a bit, but his cock pulses in my mouth, impossibly harder, so I do it again and again, slowly breathing through my nose to take him deeper.

It's an odd combination of power through submission, probably for us both. His relinquishment of control and letting me decide how fast and how deep, while at the same time knowing he could shove down my throat and choke me on his cock before I could stop him. My submissive posture on the ground before him, but knowing that I'm the one shredding his every ounce of control.

I find a new rhythm, taking Liam deeper in my mouth, sucking him fast and hard, and his abs clench under my hands. "Fuck, doll . . . I'm gonna come. Swallow it down. Swallow me."

A few more strokes, and his hot cum jets out as he grunts, probably loudly enough for Jacob to hear, but right now, I can't care because this is sexier than I'd ever imagined. His hands shoot to my head, holding me deeply, my mouth filled with his cock and his cum. I swallow reflexively, over and over, taking him in as he shudders.

I sit back on my heels, a satisfied smirk on my face. I just did that. I took the initiative to seduce him, took control and made him sit there like the nice boy he's definitely not while I worked him, and took every drop of his cum. It's quite the power trip.

Liam looks surprised at the turn of events too, maybe even shocked at my forwardness. I like that I can keep him guessing, like I'm not a pawn he's moving about on the chessboard but rather a queen in my own right, moving wherever the fuck I want to on the board.

I get up, straightening my skirt and wiping at the corners of my mouth like the lady I am. "You look like the cat that got the cream," Liam teases, a satisfied grin over-taking his face though his eyes are still a bit dreamy.

I lift my eyebrows. "I *did* get the cream, Mr. Blackstone."

He growls at my usage of his name. "I want some fucking cream too, Arianna. My driver will pick you up at seven sharp. Pack a bag because you're staying at my house this weekend."

I consider playing coy, letting him continue to chase me,

because I haven't exactly agreed to this weekend sleep-over plan. But I know I'm reaching the end of my rope, and I suspect he is too. This back and forth we've been playing at has been fun, and already so very educational, but my resolve to wait is weakening, barely a sliver of a memory about why I decided that in the first place -remaining.

"Seven it is. I'll be the one wearing . . . lace," I say, getting one last tease in because I already know how much he loves the peekaboo effect of the flimsy fabric against my skin.

I can hear the moan of desire rumble from his lips as I close the door behind me to head to my desk.

CHAPTER 8

"*O*h, my God, Daisy. What the hell have I gotten myself into?" I screech into the phone.

"Breathe, honey. You're okay," she says in a soothing voice. "Inhale. Exhale."

I do as she says, slowing my breathing. The quick ride home had found me feeling sassy and rather sure of myself. But when I started packing a weekend bag and digging through my lingerie drawer and considering whether I needed actual clothes or not, the nerves hit me and I'd called in reinforcements. "Am I really doing this? I've waited so long, decided ages ago to wait until I was getting married. Is it stupid to throw that away, give in to lust?"

Daisy hums. "Why did you decide to wait?"

Knowing I'd promised her this, I relent. "Ugh, it's a long story, but I'll try to give the quickie version. I went out with a guy in high school a few times. He was nice, we had fun, and I thought things were going really well.

Then I found out he'd told the whole football team that he fucked me in the backseat of his car on our first date. Totally not true, obviously." I sigh, the story difficult to tell but easier than I would've expected. I guess the time since then has lessened the pain to the point it almost feels like it happened to someone else, like I was someone else back then.

"I told everyone he was lying, but they believed him over me. I think they saw a nice girl with curves that I didn't know what to do with, and a popular jock guy, and well . . . they figured I'd put out and had morning-after regret. Anyway, after that, I became the joke of the school almost overnight. Other guys started saying that they'd screwed me too. I don't know why they all ganged up me, lying like that, but somewhere along the way, I figured out it'd be easier to claim it with pride than argue against a title they'd already decided fit me."

Daisy's voice is quiet as she asks, "I'm guessing that title wasn't homecoming queen?"

"No, everyone was calling me a whore, a slut, easy. Shit like that. It hurt, especially considering at the time, I hadn't even kissed a guy." A sad laugh escapes my throat. "After that, though, I became much more aware of people's relationships. I could tell who was having sex, who wasn't, and I watched what happened when they took that step. I guess I just figured out that sex is a big deal. At least to me. And I told myself that I wasn't going to do it casually. And now I'm scared I'm just tossing all that away because I'm horny."

"God, Ari. I'm so sorry that happened to you. That sounds awful. Can I tell you something though?" I murmur my agreement, and she continues but doesn't say what I expect from my sweet, nerdy bestie. "Ari, listen to me and listen good . . . fuck those people who were mean. Don't give them an ounce of power over the choices you make today or tomorrow. They already got yesterday's. Fuck. Them."

"What?" I say, shocked at the fury in her voice.

"Seriously, chica. Only you can decide if you want to have sex or not, but don't let their whispers in your ear sway you one way or the other. Listen to your own heart and decide. You never made a moral, ethical, or even a conscious decision to wait. You made that choice out of hurt and fear because of asshole people who had nothing better to do than gossip about a little girl. You could've easily become what they said you were, but in your heart, you never did, even if you mouthed about it as a coping mechanism. Let me ask you this . . . does Liam make you feel things you've never felt before? Are you going to regret doing this or are you going to regret *not* doing this?"

Her words are like a balm to the little girl in my soul who cried at the ugly words tossed so carelessly at her like bombs. Though those scars will likely always remain, I can feel at a visceral level that she's right. It's not that I'm throwing away my heart or my body on a meaningless fuck. It's that I'm finally taking my own power, giving myself permission to enjoy my body without caring what others may or may not think about me afterward. Sex is a big deal, but it's *my* big deal, and no one but me gets to choose when the time is right for me.

And though it's fast, I do feel something for Liam. It's not love—it's way too soon for that—but it's not simple lust either. This is something I've never experienced before, some combination of happiness, respect, heat, and excitement. It's both bright and bubbly and simultaneously dark and sultry.

"I'd regret not doing this. I don't know what this weekend holds, but I do want to find out. Maybe we have sex, maybe we just go a bit further than we have, but I want to take that leap, make those choices myself." I smile, a heavy weight lifted from my shoulders. "Wow, Daisy. Thank you, girl. I don't know what I'd do without you."

She laughs. "That's what besties are for. I do have one more question, though . . . what are you going to wear?"

I flop back on the bed. "Oh, my God, I don't know! My lingerie drawer is literally emptied out on the bed around me. I don't have a fancy boudoir set like Liam is probably expecting, nor can I afford that. I also don't have any slutty 'fuck me' gear. I told him lace because I was taunting him, but now I'm seriously considering running to the mall for something special."

Daisy clicks her tongue. "Ari, if he's nitpicking your lingerie, tell him to fuck himself and get the hell outta there. Seriously. The man isn't gonna care if you're wearing your time-of-the-month granny panties and a T-shirt bra or a fancy set. And you probably don't need the added pressure of some big to-do outfit. Wear something you have that makes you feel pretty and sexy. What do you have?"

"Hang on . . . let me switch to FaceTime." I click the buttons and suddenly, Daisy's face fills my screen. Even through her big glasses, I can see the kindness in her eyes and my heart swells. I'm lucky to have her. "Thanks again, girl. Okay, here's what I have . . ."

Almost thirty minutes later, I've picked out a few lingerie sets from my stash, lacy, pretty matching things that make me feel good without seeming like I'm trying too hard to be something I'm not. I add a few silky shortie pajama sets, some soft lounge clothes, and one dress that will work for a casual brunch or a nicer dinner. And with that and some bathroom necessities, my weekend bag is packed.

I'm ready.

I think.

Well, I'm definitely ready to be open to the experience, at least. I'll take it moment by moment, with no pressure from Liam, my past, or myself to do or not do anything.

At seven on the dot, there's a firm knock on my door. I open it to see an older man dressed in a black suit, a burgundy tie sharp against his white shirt. He inclines his head, tilting an invisible hat at me. "Ms. Hunnington? I'm Randolph, Mr. Blackstone's driver, among other things." There's a slightly British lilt to his voice, making him seem charming and grandfatherly. He offers his hand, and I shake it, introducing myself too.

"Other things?" I ask, not sure what he's talking about.

He smiles politely. "Driver, butler, house manager. I suspect you know Mr. Wilkes? He takes care of Mr. Blackstone's professional life. I handle his personal affairs. He said you're to go to his home. Correct?"

"Yes, that's right."

He takes my bag and escorts me down to the black Mercedes waiting at the curb. It's sleek and sophisticated, all curves and class. Randolph opens the door, waiting for me to climb in, and then closes it firmly behind me.

The ride is relatively quiet, just the purr of the powerful engine. I slide my hand along the leather seat, feeling the luxury of the buttery softness. I vaguely wonder if Liam appreciates the extravagance of this. He's told me about his upbringing, definitely wealthier than mine by far, but rather than a silver spoon entitlement, he came out of it with a work ethic not many possess. But when you grow up with money, there's an inherent expectation that goes with the experience. I hope that even when I'm a big-deal CEO, I still appreciate the special things, like a chauffeured ride in a fancy car. With a small smile, I make a mental promise to myself to eat some beefaroni at least once a month too.

I'm not sure what to say to Randolph, who seems to be taking my lead on small-talk and stays silent. But I do notice him glancing back at me in the rearview mirror, and I consider that he's probably done this before for Liam. Pick up a woman, take her to his place for the weekend, and repeat. The thought leaves me cold, but I can't fault Liam for having a past if I don't want him to fault me for mine.

I realize that Randolph is trying to figure me out. I can almost feel his judgment . . . too young, too innocent, too much cleavage, too much . . . of a whore. His eyes stay perfectly neutral though, and I have a sudden insight that the whispers of my past and my own inner monologue are filling in gaps that don't exist. Daisy is right. I am letting my past control my present and my future.

And I'm not going to let the small-town assholes or a driver in my present decide for me. I decide who I am, what I am. And I say I'm a woman with a brain, a heart, and needs. And that's okay, so they can fuck off. I sit up straighter and meet Randolph's eyes in the mirror. He offers a small smile, and I feel like I passed his test, but ironically, it's one that I don't feel the need to care about because I passed my own, which is much more important.

My mouth drops when we get to Liam's estate. It's beautiful, not a stuffy brick and stone testament to century-old dead men, but sleek and contemporary. Steel and glass dominate the whole structure, as if the architect was inspired by the pyramids outside the Louvre.

"I've never seen anything like this," I murmur as we pull up.

Randolph smiles and nods. "This way, Ms. Hunnington."

He already has my bag in hand as we approach the front

doors. Randolph pushes a button and the gigantic glass front parts, awing me as I get a good look at the interior.

Everything gleams. Rich, warm marble floors flow from room to room through open doorways. Somehow, there isn't a column in sight, and I can see upward to the evening sky through the large skylight in the foyer. It feels like I'm not indoors at all, except that my heels click on the floors as Randolph leads me through the entry area and deeper into the house. I have to stop, though, as we go down a hallway, pausing in utter astonishment. "Is that . . . a pool?"

Randolph stops, nodding.

I shake my head, amazed. I've heard of infinity pools before, but I've never actually seen one in person. Liam's pool goes right to the edge of a huge drop-off, almost like it's about to join the sky before the view opens up to an enormous valley thick with pines and other trees. "I've never seen this part of town before. It's beautiful."

"That land is actually state forest, so there is no chance of it ever being cut down. Makes for a rather spectacular view," Randolph says. "This way, please. I'll show you around."

"Where's Liam? I don't mind the tour, but I thought he'd be here?"

"Mr. Blackstone asked that I give you this." He hands me a sealed envelope, the paper rich and creamy. I recognize it from the stationary set on his desk. It's scented faintly of Liam as I open the seal and take out the folded piece of paper inside. It's his handwriting, and my pulse quickens as I read the simple message written on it.

> *I have a business dealing that's taking my time.*
> *Have dinner, and then prepare yourself for me.*
> *Tonight, you're mine.*
> *-Liam*

Randolph inclines his head, waiting patiently as I clutch the paper to my chest. "Ma'am, would you like the tour? At least to get to the kitchen, and perhaps the living room?"

I nod and follow as he sees me to the kitchen. "Dinner will be served whenever you are ready. This way, please." He then shows me the living room, although it seems more like a comfy movie theater, considering the size of the television screen and the leather reclining couch. Finally, he escorts me to the master bedroom, setting my bag on a side table. "Mr. Blackstone asked that you make yourself at home and he'll be here shortly. Pick up any house phone and dial *0 to reach me in my quarters if you need anything, Ms. Hunnington."

I nod. "Thank you, Randolph."

And then I'm alone in Liam's bedroom. The huge bed, covered with a fluffy grey comforter, fills my vision, and my blood races through my veins. Is this the night? With a soft smile, I shimmy and bounce on the bed, letting out a squeal of excitement.

CHAPTER 9

"*And* so, gentlemen," Melvin says up front, finally coming to the end of his presentation, "we should look at investing in these markets, particularly these specific companies, to insure ourselves against the predicted upcoming trade war."

I try not to roll my eyes. The board, all freaked out over rumors of tariffs and counter-tariffs and more, had insisted on this meeting. Melvin's been talking for what feels like forever, happy as a clam in mud to have the floor. He's shown us charts, graphs, and even a spreadsheet that was so convoluted I think he was the only one who knew what it actually said.

Still, it's a shame he's not the greatest at actually presenting it because his numbers are pretty on point, even if I still disagree with what we should actually do with them. "Thank you, Melvin. I know the board appreciates your hard work to bring these figures forward." He preens a bit, his smile stretching across his thin face as he makes eye contact with anyone still looking at him. As I expected, though, most of the suits around the table have their eyes locked on me, checking my response to Melvin's presentation. "I think we're all concerned about the possibility of tariffs and what the fallout could be, but they're all conjecture at this point. I have to believe, and history has shown, that we're not going to end up in a worst-case scenario situation like Melvin has forecast."

Melvin interrupts me, arguing, "But predicting the market is what I do. Something Morgan has always entrusted to me."

His tone is harsh, more sneering than I usually expect from him, and I realize I've touched a rather sensitive nerve. Framing my words carefully, both for the board and for Melvin, who has been a useful source, I say, "And you are an excellent analyst. Your team is integral in evaluating possible opportunities and pitfalls." It's the best ego soother I'm going to offer, because I quickly deliver the cutting blow. "But ultimately, it's up to the board to dictate what we do with the analysis you provide. In this situation, I feel strongly that staying our current course of action is in Morgan's best interest. We can continue to reevaluate as the tariff situation evolves, but I don't currently feel the need to preventatively safe-guard assets because the sky might be falling some time in the future if X, Y, and Z occur."

Melvin is turning a slightly ruddy color and his eyes might as well be shooting daggers. Oddly enough, I can respect that. He's a passionate and intelligent man who wants what he thinks is best for Morgan and is willing to fight for it. I just happen to disagree with what that choice should be. "It's an ongoing situation and we'll take that into consideration, but the assets you recommend reallocating to safer markets would then earn approximately six percent, right?"

Through gritted teeth, he corrects me. "Six point four percent."

"Exactly. Six point four. Where they currently sit, they're earning upward of twelve," I say, speaking to the board members. "Or, Melvin, what's the exact percentage, currently?" It's an attempt to get him to see reason, but barring that, having him speak the words that will seal the board's agreement with me is a power play.

Melvin turns to look at the spreadsheet behind him, something I know he doesn't need to do since he has these numbers memorized backward and forward. "Twelve point one percent."

"So, leaving them, even if it's only for a short time while we watch the tariff news, puts us in a stronger financial position. If our current investments decline, they're not likely to drop almost fifty percent overnight, and even if they did, we would've made more during the time at the higher return rate to offset that, and the loss would be deductible on taxes." I finish my sales pitch with a smile, softening the strike to Melvin and his presentation.

The board members nod and murmur their agreement, and I'm done with this conversation, ready to get home to Arianna. "So, I think we'll stay the course for now, with close follow-up by Melvin's group." I eye him for agreement, and he nods tightly. "I think we can call that an evening, people. Have a good weekend."

I get up from the table, forcing myself not to run from the room in my hurry to get to Arianna's sweet pussy. Melvin stops me with a hand on my arm, though. I look down, not liking his nerve. "Sir, I really think if you look through the projections, you'll see that I'm right."

I sigh inside. I have to give the man credit. He's persistent, which is a good thing, but my gut says he's not correct. It's just too soon. "I'll go back over them, but my gut says to stay the course. Sometimes, the smarter move isn't the safer move. We need big risks to get big reward, and honestly, this isn't even that big of a risk. Surely, you see that? But we'll keep a close eye, continue evaluating. I'll need you to do that, Melvin. Can you handle that?"

His eyes narrow in confusion. "Your gut? You're risking Morgan based on your gut?" At my silence, he shakes his head, blinking rapidly, and schools his face. "Okay, Mr. Blackstone. It's your call. I'll keep an eye on it and report back to the board if there are any changes."

I can feel that it's a submission on his part, but not one given willingly. Pretty sure this bridge is burned and that I won't be getting any further intel from him, I go ahead and throw kerosene on the raging inferno Melvin is hiding behind his blank face and bespectacled stare. "To me. If there are changes, report them to me. I'll deal with the board." I don't bother asking if he understands. It's a direct order so he'd best get with the program. I don't require my employees to be yes-men. In fact, I appreciate and respect general discourse about company direction. It's a team effort and that's why there is a board who votes on decisions. But someone has to take the ultimate responsibility for those calls, good or bad, and that someone is me. Morgan hired me because I take calculated gambles, and that's exactly what I intend to do.

Melvin nods, though his cheeks are splotchy with redness. "Of course, sir." His retreat down the hallway is swift, not quite a stomp, but even from behind, I can see the anger in his stride.

Jacob approaches slowly, whistling as he follows my sightline. "You shit in his cereal after already pissing in his Cheerios? That's a cold-blooded dick move, even for you, Liam."

I turn, smirking at his irreverence. No one else talks to me like that, and I'm glad to have Jacob to call me out, even if it's not warranted this time. "No, he'll be fine. Though I wouldn't expect him to rat on board happenings again." I shrug. "All right, I'm out for the weekend. Only call if the building's on fire."

Jacob grins. "Gotcha. Real quick while we walk . . ." We head down the hallway from the conference room to my office, Jacob rattling as we go like usual, and I nod along as he confirms the things he's already done in my name to handle business. "Last but not least, Helen from the magazine emailed during the meeting. She's a go for Arianna being in the photos. Apparently, she was as big of a hit with them as she was with you." He gives me a healthy dose of side-eye, but I choose to ignore it. He's made his stance clear, and we're mostly just avoiding the elephant in the room.

"Also, Helen was struck with a last-minute stroke of brilliance." He rolls his eyes before continuing. "She's throwing a cover reveal party for you on her yacht, down by the coast. Next weekend."

I stare at Jacob. "Next weekend? What the hell's with the last-minute shit?"

He laughs. "I knew you'd say that. It's called spontaneity, man. Look it up. And your calendar was shockingly clear that day, although I would've switched it up for something like this. You don't exactly want to piss off Helen because, let's be real, her get-togethers are networking extravaganzas and PR godsends. Plus, she's running it like a pop-up party, some fancy food truck chef taking over the kitchen to make lamb pops or some shit. And you want to hear the best part?" I can tell by the gleeful look in his eyes that the 'best part' is going to suck big time. "It's a costume party! Well, more like cosplay, I guess. Modern movie, game, and comic characters *strongly* encouraged."

I was right. His idea of good news is my version of hell. I don't remember the last time I dressed up in a costume. Maybe when I was eight or nine for a Halloween party? Unless . . . wait . . .does a toga party in college count? Probably, so it's been ten years at least. But Jacob's right. This isn't a party I can miss, especially if it's to reveal the cover with me on it. Jacob keeps trying to convince me as we walk into my office. "Helen is apparently a not-so-secret eccentric and loves to play dress-up. It could be worse! She had a Marie Antoinette themed party once, complete with powdered wigs. Another time, she apparently celebrated a particular movie opening with a Latex and Lingerie party. Wish we could've gone to that one." He wiggles his eyebrows exaggeratedly.

I sigh. "Okay, costume party next weekend. I'll get Randolph to pick up . . . something. Maybe I should go as Gordon Gekko after all?" Jacob shakes his head sharply, and I let the idea of an easy suit and suspenders costume go.

"I need to give Helen's people a head count. Who are you thinking? We need to make an appearance as Morgan, show support and all that." He holds his tablet, ready for me to dictate a guest list.

By next weekend, Arianna will be fully mine and ready to give Morgan a long-time shot. A great way to cap off her return to college, too.

"Me, Arianna, you, and a date, if you'd like. The board members and spouses. Anyone else you can think of?"

Jacob hums. "VPs?"

I consider for a moment, mentally tallying up the various VPs over each department and division. "No, I think that might be overwhelming. That's at least twenty more people, plus spouses. I want to be able to speak with the other people there to network, not be forced into speaking with staff I can see on Monday." He nods, letting me know he agrees with my assessment, and I grab my briefcase, shutting down my computer. "I'm out.

"Where are you going with a rocket up your ass?" Jacob asks. "I've never seen you beat me out the door before."

"Today's a day for first times," I reply, grinning, but he doesn't get the double meaning. "And I'm going home."

THE FERRARI IS A PLEASURE TO DRIVE, AND I'M HOME IN a jiffy. It still feels like too long since I last saw Arianna, though it's only been a few hours. When I pull up, I feel the thrum of the engine rumbling as the glass garage doors open for me. They aren't really glass, of course—they're laminate—but I do love the irony of living in a 'glass house', considering the number of stones I throw around the business world.

Randolph is waiting for me in the back hall as I come in from the garage, his hands behind his back and his face stern. "Mr. Blackstone, welcome home."

"Is she upstairs?" I ask, handing Randolph the keys.

"She is. After a light dinner, she said she was fine waiting for you alone. Will there be anything else tonight, sir?" His voice is even, practiced neutrality.

"No, that's everything. Thanks, Randolph," I say hurriedly, barely restraining myself from running up the stairs to my doll.

Randolph clears his throat, "Sir? If I may . . ." I look to him, seeing his request to speak freely in his eyes. I dip my chin, giving permission. "Forgive me if I am out of line, but there is something special about her. She seems strong, but also . . . fragile? Do be careful."

I don't like his insinuation that I'm some gruff asshole, but it's closer to the truth than I'd like to admit and he knows it. But I'm not sharing my feelings with Randolph, even if we have worked together for years. We're close, but it's a decidedly more professional relationship than I have with Jacob. I nod, letting him know I hear him. "Thank you, Randolph. I appreciate that, and I know that she's special."

Even the words on my tongue feel inadequate. It's only been a short time, but spending hours on end together, discussing business but also our pasts, and sharing our thoughts has been like a microcosm of rapid get-to-know-you speed-dating. Tonight is special, whether I get inside her body or not, because I'm already in her mind and she's inside mine. The mere fact that she came to my house is a step in the direction I've been pulling her toward all along.

I head upstairs, finding Arianna in the main living room, looking out through the tall windows to the treed area behind my property. She's changed, and my heart pauses in my chest as I take her glorious form in. The white silk robe she's put on both hides and hugs her form, and her long legs stick out the bottom, seemingly going for miles to her cute little bare feet.

The robe is slightly see-through, and what I can see underneath stops my heart again. I can't see the details, but the faint outlines of what she's wearing have my cock rock hard in my pants.

She hasn't heard me come in and I don't want to startle her, so I clear my throat before I speak. "Like what you see?"

Arianna spins around, her mouth going wide with shock as she sees me. "Y—you have a beautiful place."

I cross the heavily carpeted floor of the living room, nothing in my vision but her. "It's nothing compared to the sight before me right this instant."

She recovers quickly from the surprise of my arrival, heat in her eyes as she traces my body the same way I'm looking her up and down. "You like the outfit?" she asks breathily. I'm not sure if it's because she's playing the part of the sultry vixen or because she's turned on at seeing me. I hope it's the latter. I don't want some faux version of what Arianna thinks is sexy tonight. I want her, real and authentic, and perfectly who she is. Nothing more, nothing less.

Her robe is slightly open in front, and I can see just how daring her outfit is . . . and there's nothing but pure honesty in my voice when I reply. "I fucking love it."

She reaches out toward me, and I take her hand, leading her in a slow spin so I can see her from every angle. When she's facing me again, she looks up. "You look dark and handsome. Maybe a little dangerous."

I grin ferally. "You have no idea how dangerous I am, doll. But I'm going to show you." I reach down to grab the tie holding her robe closed, slowly pulling the bow undone like she's a gift. A present just for me. Her robe falls open, and I memorize every inch of the pretty picture she paints before me, dark waves of her hair swept over one shoulder, white robe framing her luscious curves, tits high on her chest in white lacy cups that let her rosy nipples peek through, and her pretty pussy hidden behind a scrap of white lace. She's angelic, pure . . . and she's going to give that to me. She'll be mine to spoil . . . but not ruin.

I pull her flush against my body, allowing her to feel what she does to me. Our bodies feel like they're merging, and I grind against her. "Fuck, Arianna. You have no idea what you do to me, doll."

"Pretty sure I can feel exactly what you think of me," Arianna says lightly as I let go of her belt to slide her robe off her shoulders. It puddles at her feet the same way my body is threatening to do.

Not yet. Instead, I run my fingers along the edges of her lace cups, tracing up her neck to run my thumb across her lips, which she kisses gently. I growl, cupping her head and entwining my fingers in her hair.

Unable to resist a moment longer, I take her mouth in a kiss, devouring her while wishing I could be soft and slow. But we've been working each other up all week and my restraint is woefully weak now that she's here and so willing.

She kisses me back, and I let my hand drop to her ass, squeezing a handful tightly and rubbing against her. My cock begs to be set free from the confines of my slacks, to gain access to her sweet innocence, so close but yet so far away.

Ari moans, and I try to guide her back toward the couch, but she resists my steps a little, putting her hands on my chest but not pushing me away. "Slow down, Liam. I . . ."

I gaze into her eyes, seeing the lust burning bright there. I know she wants me, wants this just as desperately as I do. "Doll, we've been waiting, slowly driving each other mad with touches here and rubs there. You had my cock down your throat just yesterday, and I know that hot little pussy is weeping with the need to come. Isn't it, Ari? Are you wet for me, ready to be stuffed full of my cock, to ride me until you come and coat me in your sweetness?" One thing I've learned this week is that Ari likes it when I talk dirty to her, damn-near comes from the filthy words alone without a touch, so I'm expecting her to shudder with need like usual.

What I'm not expecting are the words she whispers. "I don't know if I'm ready for this."

CHAPTER 10

ARIANNA

*M*y words hang between us, and I wait for Liam to react.

I expect him to get angry, to at least get annoyed.

After all, we have been building anticipation for this event for an entire week, a build-up I've been actively participating in, only to kill his hopes within the first thirty seconds. I mean, of course, he expected it to happen tonight. I've led him to believe that for most of the week, even as my emotions went back and forth. Hell, I came here tonight thinking it was The Night myself.

But he just stares at me for a long moment before throwing back his head and chuckling. "Are you serious?" he asks in that deep, sexy growl.

I nod, facing him with as much strength as my five-foot-four-and-three-quarters-inches can muster. "I'm not giving you my virginity. Not today, maybe not ever. I just don't know . . ." my voice trails off.

There's a flash of frustration, but he studies me with sparkling amusement in his eyes. I'm reminded of the way he examined the room at the photoshoot when we first met, as if he's above everything that's happening around him. "You're nervous. That's understandable, doll. But I'm not pressuring you here. If you want to, I'm damn sure ready to fuck you all weekend long. If not, we can sit and" —he looks around the room— "watch tv or something."

Though I know he doesn't actually want to watch television with me while I'm barely half-dressed, the thought that he actually would is comforting on some level. It makes me feel like I'm calling the shots, or at least a fraction of them. "I'm not nervous, Liam. I'm fucking terrified. I thought I could do this, that I was ready. But standing here in your fucking mansion, after being driven over by your house manager who's probably dropped off all your women for a weekend of fun, it just hit me how crazy this is. How stupid I'm being. The first time is a one-time thing and I want it to be special."

"I get that, Arianna. Don't you think I want—"

But my nerves are gaining momentum, letting my mouth run away with truths I'd probably be better served to not share. "A lowly college intern and the bigshot CEO? I mean, that's a joke. I'd be the joke. Again." The thought drops the wind out of my sails, and I collapse to the couch, pulling my knees to my chest. "This whole . . . whatever this is between us . . . is centered around you wanting one thing from me. It's a game, and I admit I've willingly played. But what happens when the game is over and you've gotten your cherry prize? You can have any woman you want. What good is someone like me to you afterward?" I shake my head, a little sad. "I made a promise that I'd save myself for the man that I'd be with forever."

Fuck. This is not what I meant to happen. Not at all. I really thought this was going to be sexy, fun, and that I'd leave on Sunday night okay with this whole thing. I try to think back to the things Daisy and I talked about, but I feel weak so I revert to my comfort zone of saying no, even as my body begs me to say yes.

Liam seems to be in shock at my outburst, like he's approaching a wild animal who might attack at any given moment, but he still carefully sits down beside me on the couch. "Arianna, at what point did I make you feel like this was a game? Have I chased you? Absolutely. And I think we've both enjoyed the back and forth of that." He eyes me, daring me to disagree, but I can't because it's the truth and he knows it. "But it's not a game to me either. I'm certainly no monk, and far from a virgin, but I can damn sure tell you that I am more interested, more invested in you than I have ever been in some one-off that Randolph drove home the morning after. Women usually just want me for one thing."

My eyes flick to his, jealousy flashing hot and acrid through me until he continues. "Not that. My money. But not you. You actually like me for some fucking reason, but you don't want me *because* I have money and a position of power. Look, Arianna . . . I don't know what happens tonight, or tomorrow, or next month, for that matter. What I do know is that I want you, and I want to see where this goes. But I won't force you into something you're unsure about. It's not fair to you, and it's not fair to me."

He leans back, and in the depths of his blue eyes, I can see that I've hurt him. I didn't mean to. I spoke what was in my heart, all the fears and doubts I'm feeling right now tangled up with pain from the past. I don't want to be that girl again, the one people looked at with an ugly sneer and called mean names.

But I never considered that Liam might have some damage too, that the golden boy big shot might not trust people lightly, might question people's motives, might feel like people think he's unworthy. Like I just did.

He gets up, walking to the window, his back to me. "Why did you come here tonight?"

I swallow at the words because in my heart, I know why I came, what I planned to happen. "Because I thought . . ." I start, trying to formulate my words. This isn't how I expected this to go at all, but I get up to walk over to him, forcing myself to look him in the eye. "You have this aura about you that makes me want to please you, but I feel so powerful at the same time. I don't know how you do that, make me feel weak in the knees but strong in spirit all at once."

The room falls silent as Liam takes in everything I've said, and I wait for him to tell me to get out.

But he doesn't. Instead, he clears his throat and leans closer. "I do. I know how I do that to you. The same way you do it to me. By giving power, by getting power. It's not an exchange, one-sided and singular. It's a cycle, symbiotic and never-ending. Perhaps I could give you a lesson?" The question is quiet, dark with meaning, and heavy with intention.

I can feel that the air in the room is changing, no longer fizzy with my anxiety but foggy with the repressed desire of our time together, as if the pseudo-argument we just had evaporated, though only part of my fears have been allayed. So maybe he's not after me for a wham-bam-get-out-ma'am fuck, but that doesn't solve the problem of what people will think.

But I still ask, "What kind of lesson?" Liam gestures toward the couch. I take his hand and let him lead me over, but we don't sit.

"Let me show you," he says, wicked promise in his voice. I bite my lip, and he spins me in place, pressing my back to his front. I expect him to be rock-hard. I'm barely half-dressed in lingerie, after all. But I find that he's soft, still thick and large but just as affected by the last few minutes as I am. The uncertainty of what we're doing together has physically manifested. He presses on my upper back. "Lean over, Arianna."

Unsure of why but doing it anyway, my mind races at the dirty position. Yes, part of my brain is rejoicing, yelling at me to spread my legs and invite him in the way I desperately want him to be. But the other part questions . . . *Why am I doing this? Why does he have this power over me?*

His hands trace down my back, light fingertips sweeping the silky skin until he reaches the dimples in my back, right above the thong panties I chose to tempt him. But then he moves his hands away, and I feel the loss of contact on a cellular level. I look back over my shoulder, watching as he reaches for his belt. He unbuckles it, slipping it free and then folding it in his hand.

"What are you doing?" Instead of the challenge I meant to offer, my voice comes out with a pleading tone, like I'm begging for whatever he has in mind.

He skims the leather end of the belt along the flesh of my ass, feeling like a lover's caress but with a mental twist that makes me pant a bit.

"You want to be where I'm at one day, right? Sitting at the head of your own company as the boss?" he asks, quiet and solemn.

I nod, though I'm not sure what that has to do with what he's doing to me right now. "I do."

"Well, let me give you a physical lesson of what it will be like on the way there." He looks me dead in the eye, giving me a chance to say no, daring me to say it. But I stay quiet. "I need your answer, doll. Yes or no."

I get it, at least a hint of what he's teaching me, already. He's the one with the belt, in charge, by all appearances. But I'm the one who grants permission, the one with the true power. He won't do this unless I allow it. My voice is strong and sure, my nerves now inexplicably silent. "Yes."

The first sting of his leather belt on my ass makes me cry out, my fingers digging hard into the back of the sofa. "That's the first sacrifice," he says, "when you have to give up that weekend with your friends to work."

He continues, never hitting me too hard and moving

around on my pinkening flesh, walking that line between pain and pleasure as the heat quickly gathers between my legs. With each lash, he names another sacrifice.

Smack. "For the lonely night off because your friends have their own lives now that don't include you."

Smack. "For the first time you have to crush the dreams and life of a perfectly fine person, simply because they're in your way."

Smack. "For the moment you realize your "friends" are just your friends because of your money."

Smack. "For when you don't know if you'll ever find love . . . because you're unable to just be you and not your fucking money or job."

Smack. "For the day you realize you'll always be alone, high in the penthouse dream of your own making, but alone nonetheless. Always alone, a meaningless footnote in an annual report with no one to share the truly important moments with or to miss you when you're gone."

My pussy is drenched, throbbing, and I'm so turned on from the naughty spanks, but my heart is also being shredded as he teaches me about pain and sacrifice. I love it and hate it at the same time, and as he smacks me for the last time, my chest heaves, my heart breaking for him. It's obvious this is what he's had to endure to achieve the success he has. I've learned more about him in the last five minutes than I probably have anyone in my life, maybe myself included. It's raw, real, and painfully honest vulnerability.

There's a long pause, and I hear his choppy breath. But then one more . . .

Smack. "For never being able to trust people . . . not even the one you want to trust most."

He drops the belt and steps back, letting me stand up. My ass hurts while my pussy is soaked, and there are tears in my eyes as I stand up and look at him, seeing more than just the sexy CEO, but the real man. He's panting at the exertion, not from the physical act of spanking but because of the work of sharing such deep truths, painfully ripping them from his heart and giving them to me.

The cycle's complete.

Though he held the belt and I bear the physical marks of that, I hold his heart and he suffers the scars of splitting it wide open for me to learn from.

Needing to comfort him, though I'm the one with the ass on fire, I reach to cup his face. "Liam . . . I'm sorry."

He flinches, shoving my hands away and pacing in front of me. "I don't need your useless and false platitudes. You think there's some perfect man, perfect moment, magic waiting to happen to give you this perfect life. It's a fantasy, a falsehood little girls imagine. I thought you were smarter than that. Life, like business, is seeing what you want and having the guts to work for it, fight for it, claim it."

I can see that though he's talking about my dream of staying a virgin for the right man, his words about letting go of a childhood fantasy are just as directed at himself. Maybe we both need to hear them.

"You'll get there eventually, walk away from this and find some poor bastard to put through all the pain and sacrifice it'll take for you to reach your dream. And then you'll give yourself to him, with all the expectations you have for that pressing on his shoulders. And he'll falter. We all do at some point. And you'll doubt once again. You told me once that the real thing is worth the price you have to pay." He shakes his head, "Today, there's no more perfect moment than now. *This* is real. But if you don't want this, want *me* enough to live in the real world and pay the price, then you should go. I'll see you at work on Monday."

His rant rivals my earlier one, both of us pouring out so much and exposing ourselves more than ever before. But his final words give me even more pause. "You'd still let me be your secretary, even after all this?" I say, shocked.

He growls at me. "Of course. Though we'll have to stay strictly platonic. My helping you isn't contingent on your giving me your body. I made that clear from the beginning. I'm not a monster, Arianna. But I think we both know you're at a crossroads, not just in deciding whether you want to fuck me, but if you have the balls for this job, this life at all. You're inexperienced in more ways than one, but I can teach you things about business and pleasure you've never even dreamed about. But only if you say yes and mean it."

His eyes float down my nearly-nude body, not pressuring me but simply admiring. I get the feeling he's memorizing me for after I leave, already certain of my answer.

I think of all the things he has already taught me—yes, some sexual, but more so how he has taken me under his wing at the office, explaining why he chooses things, helping me see the bigger picture of his decisions and plans for Morgan. And I know he's right.

He's shown me nothing but respect, challenged me to be better, and accepted my every truth with understanding, even when I flung them at him with every intention of having them slice him painfully.

I collapse to the couch, the weight of the realization heavy on my heart. "You're right, so fucking right. I have been holding on to the dream of a little girl, not one born of innocence and sweet dreams but one created in fear and humiliation. My doubts now are mostly about being scared you're going to hurt me like the boys in school did. But you're not them. And I'm not that girl anymore either. I want a life big enough that it scares me, challenges me, pushes me like you do. I need someone strong enough to call me on my shit when I break down but who will let me hold them when they break down too. Give and take, Liam."

His eyes bore into mine, and I say the words I thought I was going to say when I first got here. It's been a more twisted road than I thought it'd be, but I think we're better off for the messiness. "Yes. I want to give you my body, if you'll take it."

CHAPTER 11

LIAM

*H*er words make my heart pound, and I'm hanging on to my control by a thread. "Are you sure, Arianna? I want you to be absolutely certain. It is a big deal for us both, but I get that it's something different for you. No doubts, no second thoughts." My eyes search hers, not willing to proceed unless she's clear-headed and positive this is what she wants. I don't think I could stand it if she regretted this later.

But she looks at me proudly, no question clouding her eyes. "I'm sure. I want you. Us. This."

I cross the room to her in three strides, pulling her from the couch to gather her into my arms. Inside me, a war rages. There's a beast that wants to pound her, fuck her ruthlessly until she is covered in my scent and cum. But there's a softer side too, one that wants to lay her down and worship her tenderly, show her what it means to be claimed by me.

But good thing for me, both sides agree that I need her now. Covering her mouth in a kiss, we make commitments neither of us foresaw with our tongues. We've been teasing and building to something heated, but along the way, we've developed something greater than the sum of the little touches.

As her hands tighten in my belt loops, pulling me to her, I realize that she is just as blindsided as I am by how deep things have gotten and how quickly this has all happened. But she's with me one hundred percent now, and I'm damn sure with her.

She pulls back, her eyes dropping, and for a moment, I think she's having a flash of shyness. But then she peeks through her lashes at me. "Can I suck you again?"

"Is that what *you* want? Or what you think *I* want?" I ask, the answer important.

She smirks, the beautiful feistiness blooming in her eyes. "What I want."

I run my thumb along her bottom lip, weighing the truth of her words, and I find that she's being honest. "On your knees, doll," I command, reaching for the button that holds my slacks closed. As she lowers in front of me, I see my leather belt where it dropped to the table and lean down to grab it.

She watches me with interest. I drape it around the back of her neck, not looped, but merely resting against her skin as I hold the ends out wide.

She reaches out, taking over as she slides my zipper down and tugs my boxers down my thighs, her eyes widening as my cock emerges, the veins along my shaft already pulsing with each beat of my heart. She licks her lips in anticipation and I grow impossibly harder.

"Open up. I won't go too hard . . . yet."

Using the barest pressure on the belt, I urge her forward, and she responds, leaning in to meet the head of my cock with a butterfly kiss that sends a shiver down my spine before her lips melt around my cock, drawing me in slowly. It's amazing, her tongue finding all the right places as she teases and explores my cock, inhaling it deeply.

"That's it, doll . . . fuck, your mouth feels good," I compliment her, groaning as she hums around my shaft in reply. "I'm going to go deeper. Hold still."

Using the belt's pressure to keep her in place, I feed her my cock, sliding all the way to the back of her throat before pulling back and starting to fuck her gorgeous face, thrusting in and out slowly. Arianna reaches up, fondling my balls as I moan, watching her eyes close in pleasure as her tongue starts to dance on my shaft.

She obeys, her whimpers of pleasure adding to what I'm feeling through my cock as I pump in and out of her eager mouth, faster and faster. She lets go of my balls and reaches around, grabbing my ass and swallowing all I've got deep in her throat, making me throw my head back in pure ecstasy. Between her hands pulling me and me using the belt to pull her, I'm as deep inside her throat as I think I can be. It's exquisite, and then she swallows, the muscles working my tip. "Fuck, Ari . . . that's perfect."

She pulls off, smacking her lips as she does. "Think you can come twice for me? Once in my mouth and once in my pussy?"

Oh, my God, she is an angel. A fucking naughty one too. "Fuck, yes. I've got plenty of cum for you. Reach down and rub that sweet pussy for me. Get it ready for what's next."

Arianna grins, and between her legs, I can see her slide her bottoms to the side to slide two fingers inside before she gobbles my cock and fingerfucks herself. It's the hottest thing I've ever fucking seen, and this won't last much longer at this pace.

I feel my balls tighten, and my cock swells in Arianna's mouth. She pulls back, sucking just on my tip as she pumps my shaft with her soft hand, and I explode, growling as I ride the tidal waves washing through me. She moans, her thighs shaking, and I realize she's coming too, her fingers filling her pussy as I fill her mouth with my cum.

When I'm done, she smiles and swallows, licking her lips before smacking them gratefully. "Mmm," she moans, pleased with herself for both of our orgasms.

The belt falls from my hands as I reach down, pulling Arianna to her feet and kissing her deeply, tasting the last traces of myself on her tongue as we caress and touch each other. She hisses when my palms run over her pink ass, whimpering in pain. "Ouch."

"I'll make it feel better," I promise her, reaching lower and picking her up. Her legs wrap around my waist instinctively. "Here or the bedroom?"

Arianna looks around, then lifts a brow. "Why not both? Here first . . ."

We sink to the floor, side by side as she works my clothes off. After I kick them away, I reach down, running a soft touch along the lace of her bra cup as she lets out a tiny gasp. I stop, looking up into her eyes. "If you say no, we stop here. I won't undo this."

Instead of replying, she reaches behind her, undoing the clasp herself. She pulls the lacy bra down her arms, her breasts popping free. I dip down to kiss and suck one pink nipple into my mouth. "So pretty, doll." My words are already gruff, need thickening my voice. She wiggles and then shimmies her panties off too, lying beneath me gloriously nude.

I prop myself up and then swallow, looking at her flawless body . . . from her cute little pink toes to the curve of her calves and the swell of her thighs before her hips flare out, leading up to the rest of her, soft tummy and proud overflowing handfuls of breast. But most of all is her face, big eyes that have teased me, taunted me, and shown me the depths of her soul. Eyes that I could look into forever.

"You're everything I've ever dreamed of," I reply, leaning down and kissing her deeply.

"You too, Liam. Everything I wanted." I can hear that she's not talking about my physique, but more about my soul. It's the best compliment I've ever received.

It doesn't take long for my cock, which never sagged below half-hard, to be fully ready to go again, and I spread her legs, getting ready. "How slow do you want it?"

"Slow," she admits. "Ease me into it."

I nod and run the head of my cock between her lips. She's so wet, and both of us groan as I begin stroking my cock back and forth, covering my entire length in her slick wetness but not penetrating her. Instead, each stroke rubs over her clit, and she gasps, arching her neck to my lips as I suck and nibble the sweet skin.

Something takes over me, and I suck on her neck harder, knowing I'm leaving a mark but glad about it as my hips pump my cock over her pussy. She's so warm, and when she lifts her hips and I slip inside, it takes me a couple of inches before I freeze, looking into her eyes. "Doll . . . you're eager."

"You were about to make me come again," she admits, gasping as I pull back and thrust slowly, filling her a little more. "I couldn't wait any longer."

I draw it out, each stroke of my cock going just a little deeper than before, filling her bit by bit and making her squirm, her hunger for me making her desperate for me to speed up. "Please," she begs.

I growl. "Told you I'm gonna make you beg for it."

Before she can reply, I thrust harder, filling her pussy all the way until my hips grind against hers, and she cries out, her fingers digging into my arms. "Fuck! Ahh!"

I hold still for a second, letting her adjust to the new sensation, and I take the opportunity to appreciate how good it feels to be inside her, merged with her body as one. "You ready, Arianna?" She whimpers in need, nodding.

I can't deny her desire or my need any longer, and I thrust deep, swirling my cock around inside her before pulling back. Slowly, we pick up the pace and I fuck her faster and harder. Arianna cries out with each thrust, encouraging me with gasped words begging for more . . . for me to ruin her . . . for me to come inside her. I give her everything she asks for, pounding her tight, sweet pussy until my hips ache and my balls swell.

I groan, my cock swelling, and kiss her deeply. She gasps, her breath hot on my face as she mumbles, "Liam. Oh, God. So good."

Arianna shudders, wrapping her legs around me as her brain hazes out, and I thrust as deep as I can one more time. My orgasm hits me hard, and I cry out, Arianna echoing me a moment later, screaming my name as she comes, her heels drumming on my spine as she tries to pull me deeper and deeper into her.

Together, we fall into space, the black void consuming us, but it feels like an amazing adrenaline rush because she's right there with me through the whole trip. It feels like I come for hours, and when it's over, I've filled her so much I can feel a trickle of cum dripping out of her. I pull out slowly, and her pussy clenches around me before letting go, squeezing every last drop out of me.

I collapse on the floor next to her, gathering Arianna in my arms to stroke her back and kiss her forehead tenderly. Her body relaxes into mine but she's racked with an occasional tremor for a few moments before she takes a deep breath and turns her eyes to me, smiling. "That was amazing."

"Was it everything you thought it would be?" I ask, stroking her cheek. She's even lovelier in this light, and I'm shaken a little. After all the vulnerabilities we shared before, I didn't think this would seem so heavy, but it does. Beautifully, magically special . . . not just because it's her first time, but because it's our first time together.

"And more," she says, crawling up to kiss me softly. "And I'm looking forward to the rest of the weekend." She freezes, a deer in the headlights look overtaking her face, and I can see the questions lingering in her eyes.

"Tell me what just went through your mind, doll. Share it with me so I can carry it."

"I'm afraid the other shoe is about to drop, that you're going to hop up and say 'ha-ha . . . you're such a sucker' and this will all be some awful joke. Tell me this doesn't end here."

If only it were that easy, just a few simple words and she'd be at ease. But no, I suspect that my doll will always need some reassurances, or at least for a while, but I will happily give that to her. "Arianna, of course not," I swear, touching my forehead to hers. "I'm not running, nor am I sending you away. Honestly, I'm trying to be as much of a gentleman as I can be and not shove my way back inside you right now. I'm sure you're sore, and I don't want to hurt you."

She grins. "Fuck being sore. I like that plan."

I chuckle a bit, pulling her closer and kissing along her

skin, marking every inch of her with my lips. As I switch from my worship on one breast to the other, I mumble against her, "By the way, we have a date next Saturday."

She grins and sasses, "Oh, we do? What if I'm busy?"

That spark right there is what I want from her. What I want *for* her. To let her demons wither away in the dark recesses of her mind, laid to rest from the sheer power she now commands. But it's still a process, a give and take, and I'm not done teasing her just yet. "You'll have to cancel your plans," I say arrogantly. "Because you'll be with me at the cover reveal party."

Arianna sits up, surprise on her face. "Huh?"

I laugh softly, sitting up to tell her about the magazine allowing her to appear in the duo shots and the costume party on Helen's yacht. "So am I going as your secretary then?"

I shake my head. "No. Arianna, I want you to go as my date." It's a statement, but there's more question there than I'd like to admit. I am a fucking machine in the boardroom, hell, in the bedroom too. But this woman could reduce me to dust with a single word. That's the power she has over me.

"What are people going to say though? The people at the office are going to talk, Liam. You know that. I'm just some random girl." I can see the echoes of the cruel names running through her mind, morphing from her childhood to an oddly similar experience at work, but I would never let anything like that happen.

And I realize that while she has power over me, I have it

over her as well. Not just her body, but her heart, and I can give her this. "What people say has no bearing on what we are. You are not some random girl. You are *my* girl."

Her face lights up and then is overtaken with a sweet smile. "Holy shit, I never saw this happening, especially like this with all the emotional baggage dumping before-hand. But I'm glad it did."

She eyes me, and I agree with her. "Me too. Although maybe we stick to more fucking and less dumping for the next round?"

"Deal!" she exclaims, rolling over on top of me. For a rough start, I think the weekend is going to be better than either of us ever dreamed.

CHAPTER 12

ARIANNA

 *ear Diary,*

I FINALLY DID IT. NOT JUST ONCE EITHER. OH, NO, I SPENT the whole weekend fucking Liam Blackstone.

God, that sounds crazy to even say, but it's true.

It was everything I thought it would be and more. This past weekend, I wept tears of overload and joy, I clawed marks in his back, I was fucked to sleep and then woken up to a tongue lapping at my pussy. But I wasn't just receiving. I was just as voracious, wanting to experience everything at once and learn whatever lessons he was willing to share.

But as major as that was, and believe me, it was the big deal I'd always made it out be, the best part was what happened before and after. The talking, the connection, the realness. The sex was amazing all because Liam showed me something. He showed me that he isn't perfect . . . but at the same time, my idea of holding out for someone who is was just wasting the precious days that I have available to me. A seemingly good way to cope and protect myself when I was younger, but ultimately, an unnecessary front to hide behind that was preventing me from having an honest relationship with someone.

No, Liam isn't perfect, and neither am I, but when we're together, we create perfect moments. We created a perfect weekend filled with laughter, orgasms, and deep conversations, and that's all that really matters.

He's the real thing, and it was definitely worth the price.

I SQUIRM IN MY SEAT, PULLING MY HAIR OVER MY shoulder as I try to focus on completing my assignment, the speech Liam's supposed to make at the magazine party tomorrow night. I've already edited the rough draft once, and I know it's solid, but trusting me with this is a big leap of faith for Jacob and I want to make sure I give it my all. It's just hard to focus when my ass is still warm from the spanking Liam gave me this morning.

"You okay?" Jacob asks as my chair squeaks for about the tenth time this hour.

I nod. Liam let me in on how close he and Jacob are, but I'm not going to volunteer any information just in case Liam hasn't told him anything. Besides, our private life is just that, private, and Jacob has made it perfectly clear that as long as we're appropriate in the office, he's happy to feign ignorance for now. "I'm fine. Just trying to get this done for Liam. I might need to read it aloud to get the full effect though. Do you mind if I take a copy in his office so I don't disturb you with my practice rounds?" It's mostly the truth, though knowing that Liam is in a meeting and I could surprise him when he comes back with a little mid-afternoon fun is tempting.

Jacob blinks, then shakes his head, not buying it. "You two are meant for each other. No damn shame at all." The shit-eating grin on his face lets me know he finds the whole thing more humorous than reprimand-worthy.

I blink faux-innocently. "What on earth do you mean, Mr. Wilkes?" I ask, intentionally using his full name. "I think your dirty mind is showing." It hasn't been long, but working closely together has given us a chance to develop a certain comfort level with each other, and we've discovered we make a pretty good team, able to get stuff done and still joke around a bit.

Jacob laughs and grabs his tablet. "I think I'll run a few errands around the building and leave you to your *speech practice*." He winks and I blush.

But as he opens the door, he pauses. "Hey, Arianna?" I glance up from my screen, and his face is serious now. "I'll admit I had my doubts, but having you to help in the office has been a godsend. You really have a solid head on your shoulders and are picking things up quickly. I can't wait to read the speech. I'm sure it's great. But maybe more importantly, I think you're good for Liam. He's been my best friend for a long time, and I don't think I've ever seen him this relaxed. You make him happy, bring something to his life that's more than just work, work, work. Thanks for that."

His words are sincere and cut right to the bone. "Jacob . . . thank you for this opportunity to learn from you and Liam, both over the last two weeks and this fall, and for trusting me with your best friend. I know we seem like an odd match, and I think I'm just as shocked by the whole thing as you are, but we fit somehow. I think we're both making each other better and happier."

He smiles, and then he's off on one of his thousand and one little jobs he takes care of for Liam.

I feel a warm acceptance settle in my heart. Having Liam's best friend approve of us is something I wouldn't have expected. I guess I still figured Jacob, and anyone else in the office, would assume some rather seedy things about me if they found out that something's going on between me and Liam. It's a nice change of pace to have someone be happy for us.

That'll be an extra-big deal when I start my fall schedule because I'll still be working here, albeit part-time around my class schedule. Liam and Jacob offered me the permanent position just yesterday, and I'd squealed yes before composing myself enough to ask about the salary package. Liam had rolled his eyes and laid out the details, including a partial tuition reimbursement program if I committed to work for Morgan post-gradu-ation. I'd signed on the last page before he even finished the explanation. He'd laughingly questioned my contract negotiation skills when I hadn't even argued the pay. But salary plus help with school is a more than fair offer, and working hand-in-hand with Liam and Jacob and learning at their side are invaluable.

I feel like I'm on the cusp of something really great here.

The lessons continue, both in business and in the bedroom.

But it's been more too. I sometimes feel like Liam and I are teaching each other, that we're exploring together what this all means. We've spent every night together since last Friday when he took my virginity. There have been plenty of sexy moments, but sprinkled through that, we've created a connection that runs deep, sharing so much of our past and making plans for the future. It seems fast, and I definitely recognize that, but I'm falling in love with Liam more with each passing day. I'd questioned whether I was falling into the trap women have succumbed to for ages, confusing sex with love, but I know that's not the case here. With Liam, I truly feel that he's worth the risk, and I'm willing to give my heart just as readily as I gave my body. And no matter what, I'm strong enough to handle whatever happens.

With a shake of my head, I return my attention to the screen in front of me to print Liam's speech. I give the printer a minute to warm up, my eyes tracing along the text, starting with the speech title . . . *Dynamic Leadership for the Next Generation of Business*.

Normally, I'd print to our in-office printer, but Liam likes his speeches color-coordinated so he can jump from one sentence to the next with barely a glance. And the color printer is a big industrial monster in the copy room down the hall. "You print things a thousand and one different ways in five different paper sizes but still say 'PC Load Letter' half the time," I grumble to the machine as I wait for it to clear. While I'm waiting, I hear someone come up behind me.

"Hello, Arianna . . . the machine giving you problems again?"

I turn my head, seeing Melvin. Even though his office isn't on this floor, I've run into him every day. He's nice every time, polite and in a certain way sweet with the way he's trying to get to know me.

But there's something about him that makes my gut squirmy. I haven't quite been able to decide if he's pumping me for information because of my role in Liam's office or if he's awkwardly flirting with me. Either way, I've kept things strictly professional, intentionally directing conversations to work-based things only and not divulging anything of consequence.

But it's so hard to be mean to this guy, especially since he hasn't done anything overtly wrong. He's just odd. "Hi, Melvin. How're you doing?"

"Oh, just the usual. Pretty good, I suppose," Melvin says. "How about you? You seem to be getting more comfortable working with Blackstone."

"The job's a good one," I reply, sticking to what Liam and I have agreed is best for the office right now. "I'm learning a lot."

"I'm sure you are," Melvin says. Though his tone is casual, I can't help but feel the undercurrent of his words is snarky. There's a moment of quiet as I turn to the copy machine, glancing at the countdown timer and praying for the saving ding of the bell. No such luck, though, and Melvin asks, "What are you up to this weekend? We should grab a drink after work. The bar on the corner makes a great martini."

I glance up, shocked that he's actually asking me out. I guess maybe that answers my confusion on whether he wanted information about Liam from me or if he wanted me. Well, unless he's asking me out as a ruse to dig for info when I'm sloshed. I offer a small smile. "Sorry, Melvin. I don't think that's a good idea." I pause to let that sink in but soften the blow, not wanting to be needlessly harsh. "I'm going to the cover reveal party this weekend with Liam and Jacob and need to spend some time prepping."

His eyes widen. "You're going to that? I thought it was only board members."

Shit. I was trying to be nice and let him down easy, and now I've stepped in it knee-deep. "Yes, they invited me to attend since I ended up on the cover too and I'll be working in Liam's office this fall. A chance to meet the board members and network a bit. I'm still in college, so those connections are essential, you know."

He nods, smiling a little. "It's okay. Maybe next time, huh?"

I want to tell him to stop, that there's never going to be a next time, but I just can't. He's already down, and telling him he's got a bigger chance of winning the Super Bowl than taking me on a date would be like kicking a shivering puppy.

My printing's done and I grab it from the tray. "Oops, gotta rush this. Have a good weekend, Melvin." I intentionally don't answer his 'next time' question, figuring I've done enough to the poor guy's ego for the day.

I head back to Liam's office, setting the speech on his

desk just as he comes in from his meeting. "Ms. Hunnington, is that my speech?"

"Of course, Mr. Blackstone," I reply, picking it back up and holding it out for him.

He crosses his office, pulling me into his arms and kissing me deeply. "God, I spent half that meeting dreaming of your sweet pussy."

He dips me back, our mouths never separating, and the speech printout flutters to the floor. Before I can catch my breath, Liam has me spread wide on his desk, his fingers already teasing along my clit as he shoves my lace panties aside. "Fuck, doll. I need to taste you right now." He dives for my center, his breath hot as he rumbles, "Want to drink your orgasm down."

I can't believe how hungry I am for him. I know I'm waking up every morning in his arms, and I go to bed every night with my head on his chest, feeling safe and treasured. But right now, I need him just as much as he needs me.

Maybe I did find the perfect man, after all.

CALLING HELEN'S BOAT A YACHT IS PRETTY MUCH stretching the term to obliteration. I've seen riverboats on the Mississippi smaller than this, and I'm pretty sure if it were any larger, it could qualify as a cruise ship. The top deck looks amazing, with lights everywhere, and already, on my way up, I've seen enough movers and shakers in the business world to make my head spin.

And that's just the ones I recognize. Some are wearing masks that don't give a hint as to who's inside. With a sly grin, I wonder if that's intentional so that they can gain a bit of insider knowledge when folks don't know exactly who's lurking nearby. Smart business tactic, I think.

I meet Liam on the main deck, near the front of the boat, and he looks amazing . . . but those sunglasses. "*The Matrix?*"

Liam looks down at his leather trench coat, black pants, and black shirt and shakes his head, chuckling. "I was going for *The Punisher*." He opens his trench coat to reveal a black shirt with a skull on it.

I smirk, the devil in my eyes. "You can punish me anytime, sir."

He leans closer, whispering in my ear as he grabs my ass under the blue and red skirt I have on. "I'll keep that in mind, Ari. I'm curious, though. Why Harley Quinn?"

I lean back, meeting his eyes and letting a bit of mania into my voice as I quote the psycho badass, "*You think I'm a doll. A doll that's pink and light. A doll you can arrange any way you like. You're wrong, very wrong. What you think of me is only a ghost of time. I am dangerous. And I will show you just how dark I can be.*"

Liam chuckles. "Well-played, doll. But believe me, I know how dangerous you are." He steps back, putting a foot of space between us to rake his eyes down my body, taking in the full effect of my costume.

My hair is dark, not the usual blonde of Harley Quinn, but I pulled it up into pigtails and used some of the temporary color spray to get the pink and blue effect. Heavy makeup, a T-shirt that boasts *Daddy's Little Monster*, my two-toned skirt, fishnets, and heeled boots complete the look. Oh, and a baseball bat that I hand-drew *Good Night* on as the piece de resistance.

Though not perfect, it's obvious who I'm supposed to be, and Liam seems to like the overall effect, judging by the way he's tracing a finger along a hole in my fishnets, right at the point where they disappear under my skirt.

"We should probably get upstairs, play meet and greet with the masses," Liam says, though it sounds like he'd rather stay right here with me. He offers his arm, and I take it.

As we head up the elevator, I can't help but ask, "Are you sure?" If we make an entrance arm in arm, everyone is going to know exactly what's going on with us. I'm proud to be with him, but a tiny seed of doubt blossoms in my belly, the worry at ugly judgment coming back with a vengeance. '*She's the whore intern who's fucking the CEO*' echoes in my mind.

"Totally fucking sure," he says, his eyes glowing with desire and more. "You're mine, Arianna. The rest of the world can go fuck themselves if they've got a problem with it." I let his assertion soothe my nerves and take a steadying breath.

With Liam at my side, I can do anything. Hell, I'm learning that even alone, I can do any damn thing I put my mind to. I stand taller, letting my shoulders drop into place and my face relax into casual confidence.

The ride up to the top deck feels like both an eternity

and like it can't happen quickly enough. My heart's swelling in my chest as we emerge on the deck. Almost immediately, we're surrounded by photographers and some media people from various websites. Liam handles them all before we melt into the crowd. "Would you like a drink?"

"Sure, but just one—" I start.

"Hey, big brother!" a chirpy voice calls, and I turn around to see a girl pop out of the crowd. One glance and I can see she's Liam's sister, Norma Jean. He's mentioned her, even shown me a few pictures, but we haven't met. "I see you took the blue pill." Liam rolls his eyes at the mistake people have been making all night.

She's wearing a white skirt with a slit cut way up her thigh and a blue button-up dress shirt with poufy gathers at the shoulders. It's almost a cute outfit, if it were 1980. The sides of her red hair are pulled back in little comb clips like it's decades past too.

"Norma Jean, what are you doing here? And I'm the Punisher, not Neo. And who are you supposed to be?" Liam asks, obviously surprised to see her at the party.

"What kind of question is that?! I'm Lois Lane, of course, the best investigative journalist ever," she sasses. "Something I wouldn't need to be if my big brother told me when amazing things like a magazine cover reveal party were on the agenda. You left me no choice, and I had to finagle an invite out of Jacob."

Liam growls, "I'll kill him. Where the hell is Jacob?" He looks around, though I know he won't actually harm him for inviting Norma Jean.

Norma Jean tsks. "You should've invited me, Liam. I want to be here to cheer for you when good things happen." Her blue eyes are soft as she looks at Liam, and I can feel the sibling connection they have.

It's funny to see Liam taken to task by his feisty sister, because not many people dare give him shit for anything. But she does it without restraint and he allows it without reprimand. "Sorry, Norma. Thanks for coming, and I'm glad you're here."

She smiles, all forgiven. Then her eyes flash to me and I'm pinned in place.

Liam laughs. "How about if I make it up to you, Sis? Strictly off the record. Arianna, this is my annoying little sister, Norma Jean. Norma, this is Arianna Hunnington, my girlfriend."

Girlfriend. It feels so good to hear him say that. Any doubts I had about his affection or intentions are washed away when he tells his sister. Despite his feigned annoyance with her, he's proud of her and values her opinion. I can tell by the way he's talked about her.

Norma Jean offers her hand. "Nice to meet you. I hear we go to the same college, but what Liam here failed to mention was how beautiful you are. I'm legit jelly."

"Thank you," I reply, blushing. "Liam says wonderful things about you too."

Norma blushes back, though she playfully says, "Of *course* he does. So what are you majoring in?"

"Business, of course," I reply, feeling comfortable with her immediately. "You?"

"Journalism," Norma says, looking over at her brother. "Well, if business is what does it for you, you've totally picked the right guy. He used to drone on and on at the dinner table about stock market index changes. Even Dad used to tell him to hush and—"

"Norma," Liam growls, interrupting. "Don't."

She cringes. "Sorry, I didn't mean it like that. Just remembering how boring you are sometimes, so if she's into that, you should keep her, Brother."

Liam relaxes at my side, the sting of Norma's accidental words bouncing off as they easily forgive each other. It's adorable, and I feel like I can understand their relationship a bit better.

Norma laughs, giving me a wink. "Before I step on another mine, I'd better work the room. We'll talk later. I think I'm gonna go sneak around and see what kind of trouble I can get into. Bye, guys."

She walks off, and I can't help but notice that quite a few men watch her go, and I have to raise an eyebrow as I look at Liam. "She's quite something," I remark. "Why'd you keep her away?"

"She's a royal pain in the ass and nothing but trouble," Liam says, but it's said with love. He snorts. "You're going to love getting to know her."

"I'm sure," I reply. We move on, chatting and having a drink before the music starts.

I'm not ready to dance yet, but it still feels good to enjoy the party vibe as all these powerful people let their hair down. We're about three-quarters of the way through the room when Liam whispers in my ear. "Let's go for a walk. I need to *relax* before my speech."

I can feel the need in his voice, and I nod, taking his hand and letting him lead me down the stairs. We walk down the hallway, and Liam checks a few doors but finds them locked. I'm hunching over, like we're naughtily sneaking around, but Liam walks tall with confidence, daring anyone to stop him.

He finds an unlocked door, and we rush in, locking it behind us. The suite is beautiful, just one floor down from the top deck, and from here, we can see the whole horizon from the balcony as the setting sun starts to turn the sky golden. "It's beautiful."

"Nowhere near as beautiful as you," Liam says, shrugging off his trench coat and taking off his sunglasses. He tosses them to the bed and I do the same with my baseball bat, the odd collection on the fancy bedding looking rather amusing. "When you said you'd have a surprise for me . . . I never thought you'd be trying to cocktease me all night with your costume."

I grin, turning away from him and walking out to the balcony before looking over my shoulder. "You want to know the real secret of this costume?"

"What?" he asks as I sway my hips back and forth seductively, his cock stiffening and starting to press against the leather of his jeans. "That you have a spare I can tear off?"

"Mmm . . . nothing quite so big as that," I purr, reaching down to swish the hem of my skirt back and forth. "But these fishnets I'm wearing . . . they're thigh-highs, not pantyhose."

Liam's eyes drop low, and once I'm sure he's watching, I flip my skirt up to let him see the gartered lace tops of my fishnets.

He growls. "You're not wearing any panties, doll."

I lean forward onto the railing and wiggle my ass. The naughtiness he's awakened in me is recklessly daring him. "Come and get it."

Liam doesn't need any more invitation. I hear his zipper slide down, and a moment later, the thick, hard heat of his cock slides deep inside me, making us both groan. "You were wet for me already."

"Being . . . ooh . . . being with you has me always wet," I gasp as Liam starts pounding my pussy. "Mmm. That's it . . . fuck me harder, Liam."

He gives me a rough, deep stroke and rumbles in my ear, "You sure your little virgin pussy can handle me fucking you that hard, doll?"

I bite my lip, trying to remember that the party is just one floor above us, though it's mostly at the other end of the boat. "Yes, yes. I can take it."

"You asked for it," he says through gritted teeth. And then he unleashes on me. His hips pump and slap against my ass so hard I have to fight to keep my footing. With every thrust, his balls smack my clit, adding to the sweet torture. His fingers dig into the flesh of my hips, his thumbs pressing the dimples on my spine as he pulls me onto his cock. He doesn't vary the rhythm to keep me guessing. Instead, he just hammers into me, mercilessly driving me higher, faster than I've ever climbed.

With every grunt, I feel pure joy fill my being, and when my orgasm hits me, he slaps his hand over my mouth, muffling my screams. In the moment, I don't care about the music, the party, or keeping secrets, but I'm glad he has enough forethought to keep our private moments between us. "Liam!" I scream against his palm. "Fuck, yes!"

Liam pauses, grinding his cock deep inside me, letting the pulses of my pussy squeeze him. When my orgasm sparks out, every last tremor stilling, he starts again, his breath coming in short little gasps.

"Need you," he moans, not quite making sense but being perfectly clear all the same.

"Take me," I reply, my body already tingling as another climax builds inside me. I thrust back into Liam, meeting his cock harder and harder as we sprint toward a mutual finish, and I feel his cock swell and his hips seize. "I'm giving you everything. Give me your cum, Liam," I beg.

It seems like Liam's climax starts from the depth of his very soul as he cries out, his voice gravelly and whispered. His cock slams deep inside me, and he holds there before he comes, the heat and release triggering my own release. We're both lost to the pleasure, and I'm sure our voices rise a bit too loud in a passionate duet that echoes over the water.

I sag, my chest heaving as a droplet of sweat falls from the tip of my nose to stain the wooden decking underneath me. "Mmm . . . don't move," I ask him as Liam starts to pull out. "I just want to feel you inside me longer."

"You know you can feel it as much as you want, anytime and anywhere, doll," Liam says softly, reaching up and stroking my hair back from my face. He lifts me from my bent-over position, turning me to face him and wrapping his arms around my waist. "You . . . you're amazing, a fucking miracle I thought I'd never find."

"Just a girl in the world," I reply nonchalantly, though we both know his words mean everything. I smile widely at him as I drape my arms over his shoulders. Though there's no music currently playing, I feel like we're dancing, floating on the waves that are gently rocking the boat.

Liam chuckles. "I'm serious. When I first wanted to fuck you, I thought that there was no hope for me. No real future, just . . . money and work. Now I know there's so much more. I found someone I can trust and have by my side for the rest of my life."

I feel tears threatening at the corners of my eyes, burning with emotion. "You were wrong that first night. You said there is no perfect man. You just weren't looking in the mirror enough. You . . . you're perfect, Liam. And you have me by your side for as long as you want me."

Liam looks like he's about to say something, but then there's a knock at the door. "Liam? It's Jacob. Helen says it's thirty minutes until go time, and she wants to go over some stuff with you."

Liam sighs, chuckling as he pulls back, shaking his head. "He's got terrible timing sometimes."

"Well, he hasn't walked in on us in your office, so don't give him too hard of a time. In fact, I'm pretty sure he's been intentionally giving us some privacy and fielding people for you," I remind him. "Go, take care of business. I'll clean up a little, fix my makeup, and meet you on deck in fifteen."

Liam nods and gives me a tender kiss. "Arianna, I—"

"Liam, come on! She's about to throw a fucking tantrum!" Jacob interrupts, knocking on the door. "Seriously, guys . . ." I can hear Jacob's eye roll even through the door.

"Go," I whisper to Liam, kissing him again. "I know . . . and me too. See you in fifteen."

"That's one thing I don't envy women for," he says at the door. "Takes me ten seconds to zip up and walk off."

"Asshole!" I joke, and Liam laughs as he opens the door and slips out. I head to the bathroom and clean up. My makeup is a mess, smudged eye shadow and smeared mascara. Luckily, it kinda goes with my psycho persona, so I mess it up a bit more to make it look intentional. A quick potty stop, outfit adjustment, and the mirror says I'm ready.

In the hallway, I see someone in a costume striding quickly toward me. He's taller than me, even in my heels, but his Ted the Bear head brings him up to well above normal height. It's a cute costume, but with this late summer heat, even at sunset, the poor guy inside has to be baking and suffocating. Then again, maybe he's naked underneath . . . I think with an internal laugh.

"Hi," I greet Bearman as I head toward the stairs upstairs. He stops, turning to face me, so I do the same. He gestures toward the bat in my hand, holding his hand out. I take the cue that he wants to see it and hold it up. "It was a regular baseball bat until I got my markers after it. Made it myself to go with my costume."

He takes it from me, holding it up to the mesh eyes in the bear head to see it. Suddenly, there's a swish of air and an explosion in the side of my skull.

I fall against the wall from the force of the impact, my mind stupidly yelling that I'm a failure as a psycho badass. As if that matters in this moment.

There's another pop, and then darkness. And none of it matters anymore.

CHAPTER 13

ARIANNA

*T*he room is dark when I wake up, a dim set of lights spinning as I blink, trying to get the world to come back into focus.

"What the . . . where am I?" I slur, my voice sounding like I've had a few too many to drink. That's ridiculous. I rarely drink, and never more than a single glass of wine after watching my parents' drunken struggles. No . . . my brain aches, and I try to focus again, trying to remember. There was . . . a bear?

I try to move, but other than wiggling my arms a little, I'm immobile. Looking down, I can see black duct tape wrapping around my body just below my breasts, holding my arms tight against my body, my wrists also bound in my lap. There's another line of black tape around my thighs and then a fourth around my ankles.

"What the . . .?" I repeat, blinking as my eyes start to come back into focus. Standing across the room from me . . . wait, not a room. It looks like maybe some sort of industrial closet or something. But a few feet away is . . . the bear?

Okay, so at least I didn't dream that up.

I feel wetness trickle down my hairline and over my ear, and I shake my head. The movement both makes my headache turn into a splitting migraine and clears my thoughts. Nope, that's not water . . . that's blood.

"Who are you?" I croak. "Where am I?"

Bearman stands there for a moment, silent, but I can feel the coldness of his stare through the black mesh of his eyes. I strain my ears, searching for any clue to where I am. I can't hear anything, but I can feel the subtle motion of the water, so I think I'm still on the boat.

I always thought if I were in some awful situation, like the attacks or kidnappings you hear about on the news, I would be the type to shut down, just cower in the corner and pray for someone to save me. The too-stupid-to-live girl who repeatedly falls while running away from the chainsaw-wielding mass-murderer in movies. I never actually considered that something like this would ever happen to me. But now that I am finding myself in this nightmare, I'm not scared into frozen inaction. I'm pissed. I'm angry. I'm . . . furious.

I don't think about whether it's a smart choice or not. I just growl out, "Hey, Bad News Asshole, I asked you a question."

Bearman steps closer but still remains silent. Fed up with his act, I swallow to clear my throat and take a deep breath. "HELP! HELLLLLLL—"

He slaps me across the face, and while his costume pads the blow a little bit, my ears start ringing again. He looms over me, threatening in a creepy costume way. "Shut the fuck up, bitch!" he says, his voice muffled by his costumed head. "It won't fucking help you."

"Who are you?"

I don't wait for the answer, seeing an opportunity he didn't mean to give me. Though my legs are bound together, I'm not tied to anything, and I bend my knees, placing my heeled feet on his furry belly and pushing with all my might.

He stumbles backward, slamming into the wall with a decent amount of force. I'm sure the costume helped take the brunt of the blow, but at least I'm fighting back.

The man chuckles, reaching up to remove his fuzzy head. The light is pretty dim, but there's no mistaking who it is. The maniacal smile is new, however. "Hey, Arianna . . . got time for that drink now?"

"Melvin," I gasp, shocked. "What are you doing here?"

"What am I doing here?" Melvin asks, laughing shrilly. "What are *you* doing here? You said you were going to meet people, to make connections. The only connection I see is you being a dirty slut for that narcissistic thief."

I'm taken aback by his fury. It was obvious that Melvin didn't like Liam, especially after Liam shut down his market forecast suggestions, but this? This is utter madness. "Melvin, the party—"

He cuts me off, slapping his palm on the metal wall of the room and continuing his rant as he paces. "He's nothing! Just a spoiled little rich boy whose daddy bought his degree. Not like me. I earned mine with hard work and intelligence." He points at the side of his head to reiterate his point, but he doesn't look like the smart analyst right now. His wild eyes, mussed hair, and sweaty skin instead give him a crazy evil look. I don't bother arguing about Liam's father, who I know for a fact didn't pamper Liam and buy him any success.

He comes closer, leaning over me, but he's learned and holds my legs down this time, not giving me an opening. "He's an empty pretty boy, good for PR. And you fell for it, just like the board did. But I won't let him ruin everything I've worked for."

He bends down, picking up something from the floor, and I realize with a shiver that it's my baseball bat. There's a dribble of blood bright against the pale wood and my stomach turns. That's my blood. I'm almost certain Melvin is going to hit me again, but I'm sure as fuck not going to be a stationary target. I twist and turn on the floor, trying to get away and yelling again, "HELP—"

He doesn't hit me, though he shoves the end of the bat into my gut hard. My breath leaves me in a whoosh and my distressed cry is cut short.

But though my vocals are absent, Melvin is ramping up. His voice gets louder and louder, spittle gathering at the corners of his lips. "It should have been me as Morgan's CEO. He stole it from me."

Slam! The bat clangs against the wall, and I huddle into myself, wanting to be as small a target as possible now and figuring I need to protect my vital organs from another blow. "I'm the one with the MBA, specializing in finance statistics."

Slam! "I'm the one who's saved Morgan from financial ruin and increased our profits sixteen percent!"

Slam! "Sixteen. Percent. Do you know how hard that is? Of course you don't. But I do, and I did it."

Slam! "Me."

He begins pacing again, and I dare a glance up, watching his progress across the room and back. Distantly, I hear a beeping sound, and through the small crack under the door, I can see a flash of red light. I wonder if something is wrong with the boat, but I figure I have a more pressing threat than possibly sinking right now.

I have to do something though. Eventually, Liam will realize I'm missing, but probably not until after his speech, and I don't know how long I was out. Maybe it's been a few minutes, maybe it's been an hour. I don't know.

I search my brain. Though this is nothing like the contract negotiations I learned about at school, negotiating always has a similar construct. I hope that's true of a hostage situation, especially when I'm the fucking hostage.

I try to find some common ground. "Melvin, you're right. Sixteen percent is an amazing increase and you did a great job. I know Morgan and the board appreciated that."

He sneers, "Not likely. They didn't even acknowledge that without me and my predictions, Morgan would've been virtually bankrupt years ago."

I hear what he wants, some recognition, and try to figure out how to get that for him. "Melvin, we can tell them. They should know how important your work is. They want to know that. They need to know. We can tell them . . ."

He barks out a mirthless laugh. "We? *We* aren't doing shit. You're a nobody, a pawn that Liam plays with. But pawns can be sacrificed, Arianna."

A shiver runs through me at his threat and my eyes lock on the bat as it swings at his side with every step.

"He didn't deserve to be CEO. He didn't deserve you. I was nice to you, you fucking bitch." His eyes shift to me, hot hatred sparking in them. "But no, even when I warned you, you fell for his act too. Just like them. He's got them all fooled. But not me. I can see what he really is."

I've got to keep him talking, let him think that I'm on his side. Play the part. It's not the one I've played most of my life, but I can damn sure play it now. I let my voice pitch higher, my eyes wide as I say, "I can't see it, Melvin. I guess I'm just too young and inexperienced, even though you warned me. Please, tell me what you see in Liam. What he really is."

"Fucking useless," he spits out. For a second, I think he's talking about me, or at least about the me I'm pretending to be, but then he keeps talking. "He's an entitled brat, handed anything he ever wanted. He rolled into Morgan and changed everything, not giving a shit about the people who built the damn company. He swaggers around like a fucking rockstar, smiling at people as he stabs them in the back. But if that's what they want, that's what I'll give them."

He freezes, breath panting as his eyes lock on me. I can see that something has clicked in his mind and I know my time has run out. He comes closer, and though I thrash about, he stays out of my range. His lips spread, his teeth bared in a threatening smile. "Oh, yeah, I'm gonna smile while I set him up to take the fall for this. They'll find your body with his filthy cum all over you and know that you're his whore. Your fingerprints and his on the bat." Unbidden, my eyes tick to where his still furry-gloved hands grip the bat, leaving no trace of him. "And when he's on the six o'clock news as a cold-blooded killer who murdered the sweet, innocent intern he was fucking, I'll step in and save Morgan the way I should have before he ever came. It'll be me."

"ME!" he yells, tapping his chest with the bat tip.

I flinch at the loud sound, but when he adjusts his grip, both hands holding the bat like he's ready to swing, my body goes into flight mode. I struggle against the tape anew, thrashing back and forth to get away and screaming.

Even as I flail, my eyes close as I prepare for him to swing. For the blow that will end this all so much sooner than I'm ready for. *I'm sorry, Liam. I wanted to say I love—*

Before I can complete my thought, the door to the room bursts open and Liam comes through the door, roaring with rage. Seeing Melvin, he catches his arm, stopping the bat in mid-swing before Liam spins them both, slamming Melvin into the wall so hard his glasses go flying off. I feel hands tugging at me, but I ignore them, my eyes locked on my saving angel. Liam may be my angel, but he looks like an avenging demon as he knees Melvin in the face, Melvin's head banging off the back wall before he slumps to the floor unconscious.

"Don't worry, we've got you," a familiar voice says in my ear, and I realize it's Jacob. I wiggle against the tape restraints, suddenly needing desperately to be free.

Liam kneels in front of me, his eyes filling with tears as he sees my bloody cheek. My eyes rove his face, needing to make sure he's real, that he's really here, that this is really over.

"Oh, doll," he whispers, stroking my cheek. "I'm so—"

"I love you," I blurt out.

Liam stops, and I feel my wrists and then my arms free as a crew member slips a knife into the tape binding my wrists and cuts me loose. My arms lift of their own volition, grabbing at Liam to pull him close for a hug. I bury my face in his neck, blubbering against the warmth of his skin, "I love you. When Melvin was about to kill me, my only regret was that I didn't tell you that. I love you, Liam. I trust you, I need you, I love you."

I feel the tape holding my legs let go, and Liam picks me up, holding me safe and secure in his arms. "I love you too, Arianna. And I promise, I won't ever let anything hurt you again."

CHAPTER 14

LIAM

"*A*re you sure you can handle this?" I ask, not trusting anyone, not for a second. I eye the tiny blonde in front of me, but she doesn't flinch a bit. That's probably a good thing, but it still frustrates me.

But Ari's calm voice soothes my fears. "It's fine. We'll be good while you're gone. I promise Daisy and I will sit right here on the couch, watch a movie or two, and be safe and sound."

I take a steadying breath, knowing that she's right but fighting the instincts that yell in my mind to not leave her, to stay by her side and keep her safe. But I realize that's a lesson in futility. Ari's going to do whatever the fuck Ari wants to do, and we've established that. Oh, she'll do exactly what I tell her, obediently drop to her knees for me or run a million copies at work. As long as that's what she wants to do. Give and take, take and give. And we've found that perfect balance together.

So I leave the two women curled up on my couch to go

get ready, but I can't help but pause at the door to listen as they gossip.

"Holy shitballs, chica. What the fuck happened? I mean, I know the basics from when Liam called . . . which, by the way, when I answered your number and it was him saying you'd been hurt, I about came through the line at him." She's not the least bit apologetic about it and really had been pissed as hell at my calling until her anger had morphed into cold fear at the news.

Arianna laughs, then hisses in pain, but I force myself not to go back in. "Sorry about that. Was kinda busy with the paramedics then." I hear the creak of the leather couch as one of them moves around, then Ari speaks again. "Well, I was kidnapped by Melvin, a crazy asshole who was all butthurt at being looked over for the CEO gig, like he had some right to it that Liam didn't. He thought he'd frame Liam for killing me, but Liam came busting in and saved me."

Daisy whistles. "Fuck, girl. That's so scary." They're both silent, but then I hear the sniffles and wonder which one is crying or if they both are. "How'd they even know where you were? And what happened to Melvin?"

"Well, Melvin was swinging my bat around like a Major League Baseball player, slamming it on the walls and stuff. I guess at some point, with his swings or maybe when I kicked him into the wall, a sensor for the boat was set off. The alarm sounded on the bridge and in the hallway, but the siren was pretty far down the hall so I could barely even hear it, and Melvin was too far gone in his anger to notice it, but it led them to check there.

Liam had already realized I wasn't in the audience for his speech and knew I wouldn't miss it, so he knew something was wrong. I got lucky."

It's quiet for a moment, and I say a little prayer of thanks at how lucky we all got that night.

"Then, between Liam, Jacob, and the crew, they held Melvin down until the police got there. He's got a broken nose and a concussion from the fight. He's worse off than I am, maybe."

She lists out Melvin's injuries matter-of-factly, but I secretly confess to myself that I'm not sorry. Not in the least. In fact, I'd do it again, beat the shit out of him even worse for daring to touch a single hair on Ari's head, for using her as a pawn to get to me.

"But you're okay?" Daisy asks, the concern for her friend obvious.

"Yeah, I'm on concussion watch for a week. But it's a mild one, not too bad, considering the blows I took. I should be fine to start school on time, just have to rest until then and be careful I don't overdo it. Speaking of, I can't really watch movies. Doctor said no screen time for a bit," Ari says, her voice already getting weaker than when she started her tale.

"No problem, honey. You seem pretty wiped out. Why don't you take a nap for a bit? I'll sit right here and wait."

"Mmkay," Ari responds, and I can tell she's already half-asleep. I'm just about to tiptoe down the hall when I hear a 'psst' from the living room.

I peek around the doorway and find Daisy looking at me with a bemused smirk and a glint in her eyes. She mouths, "We're fine, go get your shit done." And then she shoos me with a waving motion of her hands. If she weren't Ari's best friend, I'd kick her out on her ass for her sheer gall.

But Ari loves Daisy, so I give her a pass. But not before telling her through a series of gestures to keep her eyes on Ari and call me if she needs anything.

As comfortable as I'm going to get that Ari is in good hands, with Daisy at her side and Randolph on extra alert, I head to the office.

JACOB IS STANDING AT THE FRONT OF THE ROOM WHEN I arrive, the rest of the board already seated around the table. "Please, I'm not at liberty to discuss what happened at the party."

Jacob's a good man and an even better friend. We knew this meeting was going to be a shit show, but I'm not one to shy away from the hard stuff when it's necessary. And this definitely is.

"Good morning, ladies and gentlemen," I say, and all eyes turn to me. The people seated around the table are all in suits, their usual office garb even though it's Sunday morning. I was too focused on taking care of Arianna to bother with dressing up, though, and I'm in jeans and a polo shirt. It's a perk of being the fucking boss. There's a murmur of greeting and I launch into what they really want to know.

"As you're all aware, there was a rather disturbing incident on the boat at Helen's party." I pause, letting my eyes click from person to person, wondering if they feel the same way Melvin did. Or hell, maybe someone here was in on the idea with him? My mind races at the thought.

John Summers, a long-standing board member, speaks out. "Liam, we don't know what happened. Just that everyone was waiting for the big cover reveal and your speech, and then we were all shepherded below-deck to the dining room. We could see that there were a lot of flashing lights, police or fire, maybe, and then we were told we could go home. We don't know anything."

"I see. Well, then let me explain a bit of what happened," I say before launching into the whole sordid tale. I leave out the part about Arianna and me fucking on the balcony, simply saying that Melvin had figured out that Arianna is important to me and was going to use her against me to have me removed as CEO.

Another board member, Susan Johansson, speaks. "I think we all knew how unhappy Melvin was with your leadership and that he wanted you fired, but I can't believe he would go to these lengths." She shakes her head disbelievingly.

I glance to Jacob, who shrugs. He caught the same slip I did. "I'm sorry, did you say Melvin wanted me fired?"

Susan nods. "Yeah, he kept bringing me all these reports, piles of statistics showing what he called your 'steady chipping away at Morgan's greatness'. Honestly, I felt the figures showed you turning around the divisions you're working on and the appropriate reallocation of resources from areas you said we should discontinue. The figures showed exactly what they should have based on your plans. But Melvin just didn't see it that way."

The other members nod, muttering things like 'he did the same to me' and 'could not get him to shut up about a zero-point-three-percent change.'

"Let me get this straight. Melvin Jackson has been coming to each of you, complaining about my leadership and trying to turn you all against me? How long has that been going on? Since I shot down his market predictions presentation?" I ask, surprised, though I should've seen this coming.

John leans forward. "It began before we even hired you as CEO. He applied for the position too, and because he's a VP with a finance background, the board interviewed him. We felt his approach was too conservative and wouldn't create the boon we knew Morgan needed to get back to where we once were. Your way is sometimes uncomfortable for us traditionalists, but we can't argue with results."

My head spins, and I begin to put the pieces together. There's so much I should've seen with Melvin, obviously. But he hid it so well, none of us realized what was lurking beneath the surface of his nerdy exterior.

"It seems Melvin is more of a master manipulator than any of us gave him credit for. He's been coming to me since day one, offering intel on each of you, saying that the board was questioning my decisions, regretting bringing me on, and actively working to renegotiate my employment contract. That stopped, of course, after I shut him down on his market forecast presentation. But I think the seeds of doubt had already been planted and watered by then, drummed up on gossip, rumors, and lies."

I glance around the table, seeing the same realization dawning in everyone else's eyes. We've been duped . . . badly. And not only did I almost lose my position of leadership here, but I almost lost something much more precious. Arianna.

"I think we're going to need to start over in a lot of ways. Though the business decisions we've made under my time here are working and Morgan, Inc. is doing better, I want the partnership between me, as CEO, and each of you, to be transparent. It sounds like we have a lot to discuss."

EPILOGUE

ARIANNA

I'm bundled up against the cold as I step into the lobby, but I immediately begin unraveling my scarf as the heated air of the building warms me. Striding through the echoing front area, I hear my name.

"Good morning, Ms. Hunnington. How are you today?"

I turn, seeing Dora Maples smiling warmly at me as she heads over with a cup of coffee. "Good, Ms. Maples. Any Christmas plans?"

She launches into a story about her kids coming home for the holiday week, and I smile, nodding along. It's nice to listen to her, chatting casually and comfortably as I walk to the elevator.

It hasn't always been this easy. Right after the whole thing with Melvin, word got out almost instantly that Liam and I were sleeping together. The rumors were pretty ugly at first, but I'd already been through that once before, so with Liam's support this time, I handled it with my head held high.

When we let it be known that we were not some casual fuck but rather a happy couple, it seemed to help after a bit of cattiness about our age difference, albeit not too much, and drastically different financial statuses. But who cares about a number, whether it's years on this earth or dollars in the bank? Definitely not me.

It took some time, but it's all died down now and most people have accepted that I work for Liam and Jacob part-time and that Liam and I are a couple. It's nice to not have to hide anymore, although we still have to sneak when we have a quickie at the office.

People are accepting, but not *that* accepting. Well, except Jacob, who just rolls his eyes.

"So, how were finals?" Jacob asks when I get upstairs.

He's bundled up against the chill, wearing perhaps the world's ugliest Christmas sweater, but apparently, it's his tradition. I guess it does help add to the festive mood.

"Kicked ass. Come on, you and Liam have been giving me enough lessons that I should be able to pass *Advanced Modern Business Theory* with my eyes closed. Hell, Liam could teach the class!"

Jacob laughs, nodding. "Well, some would call that an unfair advantage . . . but that's what business is all about." He checks his desk, humming. "Hey, Helen sent over a few copies of the magazine. It hit newsstands already, but she wanted you to have a few for posterity. Her words, not mine."

He hands over a stack of six magazines, and I trace the photo of Liam and me on the cover. That seems so long ago. Just an overworked and underappreciated intern who got roped into something wildly beyond her dreams and ended up with the perfect man.

The one worth waiting for, the one worth paying the price for the real thing. The one I love. "Hey, where is he?" I ask, thinking that Liam's schedule had an early morning meeting, but he should be in by now.

"You should keep up with your boss's schedule better, Ms. Hunnington. That is your job, after all, right?" I hear a voice say behind me, the laughing arrogance sending a shock through me the same way it does every time. He's not a fairytale Prince Charming, that's for damn sure, but he's my Mister Right . . . and my Mister Right Now.

I spin in place, looking up at Liam through my lashes and clasping my hands behind my back. "You're right, sir. I'm so very sorry. Perhaps you should remind me again about where to find your . . . *calendar*."

Liam growls and grabs my hand, dragging me into his office. Right before he shuts the door, I hear Jacob call out, "I guess I'll be holding your calls?" Liam's answer is the click of the lock on the door.

"Such a naughty doll, forgetting about my calendar," he teases, letting his voice drop down low as if he's reprimanding me. "Strip for me. Get against the glass."

I obey, but slowly, taking my own sweet time to give him what he wants. I slip my heels off, lay my skirt and blouse over the back of the chair, and then give him a questioning look.

He's already rubbing his hand over his thick cock, the thin fabric doing nothing to hide how hard and swollen he is. "All of it, Arianna."

I reach back and unclasp my bra, setting it on top of the stack of clothes before sliding my lace panties off and doing the same with those.

I take deliberate steps to the window, knowing that he's stroking himself as he watches me. Once I'm there, only then does he follow me over. He crowds against me, pushing my overheated flesh to the cool window, his cock nestled against my ass. "Don't worry, doll. No one can see you but me. But I want to fuck you overlooking my kingdom."

I have a flashback to when he discovered me sitting in his chair, thinking it was fit for a king and that he was definitely the man in charge. He still is, and now, for as long as I let him be, he's in charge of me too.

"Put your hands on the glass and arch your back for me," he says, and I gladly obey that order, knowing he's about to give me what I want. I hear his zipper being lowered and then him moving about as he stacks his clothes up on the chair with mine.

Sometimes, it's a wild tornado of flung-off clothes with us, but this deliberate stall while I wait for him is so fucking sexy. The way he plays me the same way I did him. Both of us knowing what's coming and letting the anticipation build.

Finally, he's behind me again. Our entire bodies connect, skin to skin and heart to heart. He crouches, and I lift to my toes, letting his cock line up with my pussy as he slams in with one thrust. "Ahh, fuck, Liam!"

And suddenly, I'm complete. Like I walk around all day, missing a piece of myself, and when he's inside me, I'm everything I should be.

His virgin.

His whore.

His.

He thrusts again, slow but hard, hitting deep inside me on that secret spot he knows makes me come in moments. His pace picks up, pulling all my attention, and my eyes flutter closed. I feel him grabbing at my hands, holding them to the cool glass and interweaving our fingers.

"Open your eyes, doll," I hear him say from far away.

Somehow, I do, blinking at the view of the city below us. Something tickles my finger, and I look over, seeing him twisting a diamond ring on my left hand. He somehow slipped it on without my realizing it.

His thrusts never stop, slowly and steadily driving me higher as my heart explodes in light. "That's it, Arianna. You're mine, and I'm going to fuck you over *our* king-dom. My dream, my reality, your dream, and now your reality. Look out and see everything I'm giving you."

I cry out, so close to the edge, but I fight the orgasm back, tilting my hips to let Liam slip out of me. I spin in place, putting my back to the window and cupping his face. "Liam, I want to see the most important thing you're giving me." My eyes lock on him, all I'll ever need, and I kiss him hard, our lips slamming together.

And when he enters me again, I keep my eyes open, never leaving his for a moment. I watch the orgasms get closer and closer, the pleasure and the love mixing in his eyes the same way I know they are in mine.

And we come together, the waves crashing over us, as sparkles dot my vision. But our eyes never close. Together, giving and taking everything.

Liam

CEO Playboy Ends Chaotic Year With Proposal to Student Girlfriend! I read, shaking my head. It's Norma Jean's second cover story for the student paper, the first being her exposé on the incident aboard Helen's yacht. "Seriously?"

Arianna, who's lounging on the other end of the couch, chuckles. "Read it, honey. I want to hear how your little sister describes you this time."

Rolling my eyes, I clear my throat and begin. "Taking her side, I see. Okay, well . . . *breaking rules and breaking hearts has been hot-headed CEO Liam Blackstone's MO since he first stepped onto the corporate scene. But now it seems the notorious womanizer* . . . I'm so gonna have to have a talk with Norma," I mutter, not flattered with her description of me. "I'm not notorious, and I wasn't a womanizer. I just . . ."

Arianna can barely contain her grin. "No worries. Whatever *experience* you had before me just meant that you could be a good teacher for me." She winks at me sassily, a habit she's picked up from my sister. They're friends now and spend way too much time chatting on the phone and giving me shit. "As long as I'm the only one benefitting from that experience now . . . and always."

I can hear the possessive threat, which should probably scare me but instead is sexy as fuck. I like that she claims me, because I damn sure claim her back. I've even threatened to make some appearances at her university, mostly so that the assholes there know to back the fuck off.

"But there might be some truth to the hothead part. Keep going," she says, and I realize that she might have a point.

I give Arianna a lighthearted scowl, but I can't be mad at her. The sparkle of the diamond on her finger is still too new. It makes my heart go soft and my dick go hard in about three seconds flat. "Let's see . . . ah, here's a part you'd like. *The couple plans to celebrate their engagement with a trip to the coast, where they'll begin a week-long cruise aboard a private yacht. Though rumors initially ran rampant about the couple, considering their age difference and the fact that Ms. Hunnington was an intern at Morgan, Inc., an anonymous insider stated that everyone is truly happy for the newly-engaged couple.*"

"Anonymous insider? She's got people at work talking to her about us now?" Ari exclaims.

We look at each other, then both say, "Jacob."

I chuckle, and Ari growls a cute little kitten sound. "Sounds like I have something to talk to Mr. Wilkes about when he comes over for Christmas dinner. Keep it professional? Indeed."

"I predict that when you yell about it, Norma Jean is going to take his side and say that it wasn't him. Protecting her source and all. You'd be better served to give her the scoop on him . . . turnabout is fair play, after all," I tell her.

She grins evilly. "Ooh, that's twisted. I like it. Okay, here's the plan . . ."

And Arianna is off and running, her plan to jokingly get back at Jacob ending up as a rehash of the Christmas dinner menu we've already discussed umpteen times.

"It'll be fine, doll. It's just the six of us, and I don't think anyone is that picky," I say, hoping she'll relax.

This is her first time to plan a dinner like this, though I've told her it'll probably be the first of many, and it's Christmas Eve, not Christmas Day, so the pressure should be lessened. But she's excited to have Daisy, Connor, Norma Jean, and Jacob over. She'd wanted to ask my dad and stepmother as well, something I think Norma Jean had suggested, but I'd vetoed that quickly. I just want a nice meal around a sparkly tree, with the people we love and who love us back. She'd easily given in, wanting the same thing and understanding since she didn't want to invite her parents either.

And then Christmas Day, it'll be just the two of us.

The real thing.

The cycle complete.

I've given Arianna my heart, and she's taken mine.

Thank you for reading! Silk and Shadows, The Virgin Diaries Book 3 on Amazon Now! And if you missed the first book, get Satin and Pearls!

Continue on for a preview of Dirty Deeds.

Join my mailing list and receive 2 FREE ebooks! You'll also be the first to know if new releases, sales, and giveaways.

PREVIEW: DIRTY DEEDS

Prologue
Shane

I lean back, keeping an eye on the club from my position near the wall. On the far side of the club, Marco the bartender is mixing up a pitcher of margaritas for one of the tables while looking cool as a cucumber in his dress shirt and vest, the sleeves on his cranberry-colored shirt rolled up to just below his elbows. Seeing me, he gives a little salute with two fingers. I return it, knowing that within a few minutes, I'll have some refreshment myself.

"Hey, Shane, you want to switch?" Nick, the guy I have working the door right now, asks. "I gotta piss."

"Yeah, I'll cover the door for a bit. Just hurry. I want to do a walk-around."

"No sweat," Nick says, heading toward the back. I take

over the door, leaning back in the stance that allows me to keep an eye on the floor while still keeping the door under control.

Nick takes his time. He always does, which is one of the reasons I'm the bouncer in charge here, but I'm not upset as I see a tight, petite blond make her way toward me. "Hey, Shane," she says, handing me a big beer mug filled with Coca Cola. "Marco said you were looking thirsty."

"Thanks, Meghan. You doing okay?" I ask, taking a moment to appreciate the wide-eyed cuteness that is Meghan. She's only been here about a week, but there's something about her that draws my eyes to her again and again, and not because I'm doing my security job. "No troubles with the tables?"

"Of course not," Meghan says, giving me that shy, sweet-girl smile that I've started looking forward to. "Actually, I've got a friend coming in later. Uhm, if a tall knockout chick comes in asking for me, you mind pointing her my way?"

"Sure enough," I promise her, an unfamiliar smile crossing my face. I almost never smile at work, but Meghan seems to pull them out of me without even trying. "You two gonna discuss cookie baking or something?"

For a split second, I see the most beautiful shade of pink as her cheeks blush, but then she ducks her head shyly. "No, she's just having a tough time with a guy she's seeing and wants my advice. I think she mostly needs girl talk, you know?"

"Sure," I lie through my teeth. "I'll keep an eye out. Be safe out there."

Meghan nods, sashaying away. She tosses her hair back over her shoulder, her hips hypnotizing me with each swing left and right. On her, the sexy moves seem unintentional, not a practiced performance like the other girls here. Nick comes back and I drain my Coke before patrolling the floor. It's not really needed, but letting the customers have a silent warning helps stop about ninety percent of the shit that can happen around here before it even starts.

As I move around the floor, my eyes tick back to Meghan as she works her tables. It's almost like I'm circling her, edging ever so closer, tempting fire and keeping the best view of her that I can. Her uniform miniskirt hugs her tight ass like it was painted on her, and as she bends down to put a pitcher of beer on a table for six, I swear she's showing off especially for me, popping her ass out in a fantasy-come-to-life move.

Maybe it's just me, or maybe it's Meghan's natural charm, but I can't help watching every move she makes. The way she licks a thumb when she splashes something on it, the way she shows her cleavage as she moves in her uniform bustier corset . . . it's all so damn seductive, and the contrast between the shy girl she is around me and the sex kitten she acts like while working makes me wonder which is more real.

Meghan straightens up, turning and looking over her shoulder at me, adjusting those thick-framed 'nerdy' glasses that push her from cute to hot as fuck. She seems surprised to find me watching, her eyebrows lifting behind the frames, but I catch her biting her lip to hide the little smirk tugging at her mouth. She's fucking with me, she's got to be. I have to hold back a growl as she goes over to her next customer, striking a pose beside the table as she takes their order.

I'd never let any of the fucknuts who frequent this place lay a hand on one of the girls, but I keep a special eye on Meghan. It makes some of the long shifts a bit easier, and stocks my spank bank with plenty of imaginary material . . . Meghan bent over the bar as I take her from behind. Or maybe twirling around a pole in one of the private rooms just for me. The dangerous fantasies are the ones where I picture her in my bed . . . hair a mess with flushed cheeks, wearing nothing but the smile I just put on her full lips.

I alternate door duty with Nick, letting him do the next floor sweep per protocol. A static position sometimes makes me antsy. But for right now, I lean against the doorframe, appreciating the best view of Meghan in the house.

I continue my scan of the room, checking customers, the bar, and the stage, but my eyes always return to the tiny, sweet blonde that is slowly driving me insane. "God damn, what I would do to you if I had a chance," I whisper to myself, knowing the heavy rock music will obliterate the words before anyone can hear them. Still, as if by some form of ESP, Meghan taunts me, crouching down with her ass near her heels to hear a guy's order. He's looking straight down her bustier at her tits and I have to hold myself back from beating the shit out of him just for looking at her. My restraint is rewarded as she rises back up, shifting her skirt back into place and giving me a bigger peek at the curve of her ass. She heads towards the bar to turn in the order, but I see the way she peeks over to check if I'm watching.

Two can play that game, little girl. I casually reach down and adjust my cock, my face hard and stoic as I give her a disapproving look. She squeaks I think. I can't hear it, but the way she jumps a bit and her mouth flies open, I imagine the shocked sound coming from her throat. I laugh to myself, but I'm not sure if she won that round or I did.

Still, I keep my cool, keeping myself under control as the night wears on. Meghan's friend shows up right before closing time, and the two have a long sit-down talk while Marco and I finish up the cleaning.

"Thanks, Shane," Meghan says as they get ready to head out the door. Her friend's gone off to use the ladies' room, and it's just us for a moment. "I always feel . . . good when you're around."

"I just want to make sure you stay safe," I reply, looking down into her adorable face. "After all, this is a gentlemen's club."

Meghan chuckles and looks around. "Not too many gentlemen in this club. But I'm glad there's at least one. Thanks again, Shane."

My name on her lips is a tease that makes me want to taste her mouth as she says it again. But her friend comes out, and the two of them leave. Meghan gives me a little finger wave as the door closes. Oh, my sweet little innocent one . . . if only I were a gentleman.

If only.

I'm anything but, which is why it's safer if you stay away from me.

MAGGIE

"Hey, Marco! Can I get a pitcher of Miller Lite for table fifteen, please?" I yell over the throbbing bass of the music in the club . . . and get ignored again. "MARCO!"

He looks over and gives me a half-understanding nod before grabbing one of the plastic pitchers and filling it with . . . well, fudge it, it's beer at least. I roll my eyes, frustrated that I have to drag the bartender's eyes away from the stage. He's been here for years, and you'd think he'd be immune to this after seeing dancers for hours five nights a week.

But he isn't. Obviously, as evidenced by the way he's staring at the stage. He moves a hand, and I think he's going to adjust his crotch, but instead, his hand lifts to his head and he slicks his already meticulously coifed hair into place. In my head, I nag him. Adjust whatever you need to, your crotch or your hair or your suave designer clothes. Just do your dang job so I can do mine. Not too much to ask, is it?

"Here you go, Meghan," he says, sliding the pitcher the last few inches to me. I notice that he doesn't apologize that he's ignored the order I placed on the bar five minutes ago, nor that the delay will likely affect my tip, not his. His eyes still haven't left the show onstage either. Such a butt-nugget.

With a sigh, I turn to see what's got Marco so blasted distracted at the moment. I know from the music that it's Allie's turn on stage. Besides being one of the people I can call a friend around here, she's an amazing dancer, definitely too good to be stripping in a place like this. I watch as she spins around the pole, her legs splayed wide in the splits for several rotations as she flips her head around, making eyes at a guy in the front row.

In a flash, she pulls her legs in smoothly, locking them around the pole and lying back in a death-defying back-bend move that puts her eye-level with her prey, although she's upside-down and his eyes are locked on her boobs, not her face. I see her smirk and then kick her legs over, rising to stand tall in her high-heeled red stilettos. It's impressive, even from just an athletic point of view, although I'm sure most of Allie's fans aren't really interested in how much she's had to train and work for her unworldly strength, balance, and flexibility.

The guy picks up a green bill from the stack in front of him, and Allie slithers down to take it, blowing the guy a kiss with her plump, heavily lipsticked lips, knowing she'll have the whole pile before her time onstage is up.

I clap loudly, cheering her on, knowing that the cash will help her out with her debt situation. She's a nice girl, my best friend in this club, and still way too good for this joint.

Still clapping, I don't hear Marco approach. "She's

something else, isn't she? Even you can't keep your eyes off her. Can you blame me? Unless . . . that's your thing?"

I laugh, glancing over at him to see a questioning look in his dark eyes. He seems more excited about the idea than I would've expected because he knows me better than that. I shake my head. "You know I don't swing that way, but I can appreciate talent and hard work. Especially in my friends."

"Calm down, Little Miss Goody-Two-Shoes. You know I'm not going near that chick with a ten-foot pole. I like my dick where it is, thank you very much."

I narrow my eyes at him, attempting to appear threatening, but we both know it's not the threat of my tiny little librarian-looking self that has him shaking in his Italian loafers. It's that our boss has taken a rather obvious interest in Allie lately. And no one dares go against Dominick if he's even considering marking some of that territory for himself.

"If you're still interested, your Miller Lite is getting piss-warm and table fifteen is looking mighty thirsty," he says, smirking. "I guess they're not into Allie. They seem to be paying more attention to their beers and their MIA waitress."

Shishkabob! My tip is definitely going to take a hit on this table if I can't turn it around with a little extra sugar. Hoping that maybe they like nerdy girl-next-door types instead of out of this world exotic beauties like Allie, I fluff my girls up in the black bustier that serves as the top half of my uniform and grab the pitcher to walk it over.

"Here you go, fellas. Didn't want to interrupt your view of Allie's special talents," I say, going heavy with the flirty innuendo as I lean over, confident that while my full cleavage is on display, they're locked solidly in the cups and won't spill out for an unintended nip slip.

Not that anyone would mind. Except me, of course. Petals from Heaven may be the sort of club where the female persuasion exposes their body parts to the spot-lights, and my uniform is decidedly sexier than I would choose myself, but I've never felt like I was expected to do more than deliver drinks. Unless I wanted to, which I definitely don't.

The guys' eyes all lock to my chest, same as always, and their eyebrows lift. Gotcha, boys. So Allie isn't their cup of tea, but I am. Well, it takes all types, and it's sort of encouraging to know that a girl like me can be compared to a goddess like Allie and sometimes get the nod. Maybe my tip won't be so bad, after all.

I take a moment to pour each of the four guys a mug, feigning a lack of skill that makes the suds at the top spill over the lip and down my hand, the white foam looking decidedly like something more seductive than beer. I might be kinda innocent, but I'm not as schoolgirl inno-cent as I look, and I know how to tease.

I give the last guy his drink and then casually lick the bubbles from my fingers, letting my pink tongue curl out before sucking a tip into my mouth. All four guys' jaws drop at my innocent display before the one closest to me grabs my hand.

His blue eyes flick up to me as he holds my hand in a near-crushing grip, grinning drunkenly. "Let me help you with that."

Before I can say yes or no, he moves forward, his blond hair falling into his face as he quickly swipes his tongue against my finger and sucks it into his mouth. *Fudge! Danger, Will Robinson. Need to back this play up without causing a scene.* One of the hallmark rules of working in a club— don't cause a scene unless you really, really need help.

Instead of freaking out, I give my best girly giggle, jerking my hand back and squealing. "Ooh, that tickles!" I laugh as I shake my hand loose. "You shouldn't be so naughty!"

"Honey," Blondie says, half getting up, "if you want to see naughty—"

Out of nowhere, Shane appears behind me. He's part of Petals' security team and the star of too many of my midnight fantasies to admit. I can't see him, but I can feel his presence like a physical force pressing against my body. It's comforting, a little scary, and also frustrating. I can't help it, Shane's just . . . well, he's as sexy as choco- late cake, and probably just as dangerous for my health.

Shane growls, his voice low and dangerous. There's no weakness, no compromising with that voice. Fact is, Shane's not afraid of anyone or anything. He might be the only person in the club not afraid of Dominick. "No touching. Or I'll be the one touching you."

The threat is apparent, and the guy's face shows his fear that Shane will kick his ass. Shane's words have the opposite effect on me, though, and my mind is filled with an image of him touching me, his strong, thick fingers tracing lines along my private silky areas, teasing and tantalizing me before taking me roughly.

Back in reality, finger-sucking guy has his hands up wide, backing down immediately. "No problem, man. Sorry, won't happen again."

Shane lets out one more growl before stalking off. I never even made eye contact with him, but under the slip of dark denim they call my miniskirt, my panties are soaked from being that close to him, having his voice wash over me, and that flash of fantasy.

Needing to save the tip, though, I smile at the forward guy, and he does at least offer an apology to me, a rarity in this place. "No problem, honey. Security is just really protective of us. I'm sure you understand."

"I can certainly understand why," he says as his eyes float down my body, taking an extra moment on my chest, my crotch, and the length of my legs sticking out of the skirt before tracing back up again. Despite my petite height, this slip of a skirt combined with my heels make my legs look a mile long, and it feels like it takes him forever to uncomfortably peruse every inch. "We're good for now, but keep the pitchers coming all night."

He says the last part in a filthy little cadence, emphasizing every word, and I can hear the obvious double-entendre. I nod and giggle, reverting to my innocent girl shtick as I promise to keep them coming.

I walk away, smiling as I hear the guys start loudly talking to each other. Two can play that game, and we're both hoping to get lucky, just not in the same way. Tip me, tip the stage girls, and get out so I can get some fresh meat at my table with another full wallet.

It sounds crass, even to myself, but it's the reality. No one is coming to Petals from Heaven strip club to find love, and really, no one is coming to find sex. Well, I guess some of the guys do come in with the fantasy of having an amazing night with a woman who ticks all their mental boxes, but the odds of that are worse than winning the Powerball.

I don't really get it. Guys crowd in with their other guy friends, pay fart-tons of money for cover, drinks, and tips, then go home to flog their bishop? Why the game? Just watch some porn or something and take care of business.

Unless the guy is paying for a private show, where they're not supposed to whip it out, but according to my dancer friends, they pretty much know they've got a fifty-fifty chance that they're going to be dancing while the patron gets down to business.

Ew. Just gross.

I make another round of my tables, getting refills, flirting, dropping off checks, flirting, collecting cash . . . and more flirting.

As I work, I keep an eye out for any patrons who might be . . . somebody. That's my real job, scouting for celebrities, major or minor, politicians, CEO bigwigs, Instagram-famous people, or anyone else who might be interesting and tends to frequent this particular club.

On one hand, they're usually the best tippers. On the other, they're why I'm really here, working as Meghan, a cocktail waitress at a strip club, undercover for the tabloid gossip rag I work for. Neither job is my dream come true, but since no one is knocking on my door to write for *The New York Times*, online trash talking pays my bills.

I got the assignment to get a second job at Petals two months ago, and to my surprise, they hired me right away. Petals is known for being exclusive and VIP-preferred, so I'd been nervous about their hiring plain Jane me. But I'd been hired as a waitress on the spot based on my resume and my other . . . ahem . . . assets. So far, the undercover gig has paid off in a couple of smaller celebrity-sighting stories, but I feel like there's something bigger here. I just don't know what it is yet.

But Petals from Heaven is sort of the place to go if you're a celebrity who wants a taste of the salacious life but you don't want to get caught out on the town because of your wife, your girlfriend, or just your reputation. There's a sense of discretion at Petals, and Dominick fosters that, making sure the A-listers get what they want, whether it's private rooms or flashy top-notch service. Plus, Petals employs some of the most beautiful dancers I've ever seen in my life. It's almost artistic, just nearly naked too. With this combination, something gossip-worthy has to happen eventually, and I want to be here to report on it.

Ironically, this undercover gig is pretty sweet and is

paying more than half my bills now anyway. It was an odd realization that the writing and research I love to do and went to school for are actually less financially rewarding than playing airhead and slinging drinks.

Not sure what that says about our society, but it's not anything complimentary.

I hear the DJ talking loudly over the mic, adding some hype to our last performer of the night and telling everyone in the club to get their last drink and get the fudge out. He doesn't use those words, of course, but I censor them in my head like I sometimes do.

I drop one last pitcher and the check at Finger-Sucking-Guy's table and he clears his throat. "Uhm, hey, so I don't wanna piss off the bouncer or nothing, but what are you doing tonight? Wanna party?"

I forcefully contain my eye roll, choosing to twirl my hair around my finger and kicking my voice up an octave. I deal with this at least once a week. Can't get the dancer, go for the waitress. "Oh, no. Sorry, honey, I can't. I've got school in the morning, so I'd better be a good girl and get home."

The reality is, I've been out of school for over three years, but they always believe this excuse because I look a lot younger than my twenty-five years. I still get carded when I buy wine.

Luckily, he takes the refusal gracefully, or maybe he's worried about Shane showing up again. "Mmm. Yes, you should be a good girl. Get right to bed."

It's still flirty and slightly sleazy, but at least he's not arguing with me. I give a wink and turn, flouncing off to close out my other tables.

Once everyone's gone and the club is cleaned up, I head backstage to change. Pulling on sweats and a long-sleeve T-shirt, I'm thinking of only a few things. Mainly getting home, taking a good long shower to get the leftover smell of the club off me, and then collapsing into bed. After all, I've got to be ready for work at ten . . . and my boss hates it if I'm late.

Get the full book here or visit my website - www.LaurenLandish.com

ABOUT THE AUTHOR

Join my mailing list and receive 2 FREE ebooks!

Other Books By Lauren

The Virgin Diaries:
**Satin and Pearls | | Leather and Lace | | Silk
and Shadows**

Irresistible Bachelors **(Interconnecting
standalones):**
**Anaconda | | Mr. Fiance | | Heartstopper
Stud Muffin | | Mr. Fixit | | Matchmaker
Motorhead | | Baby Daddy | | Untamed**

Get Dirty **(Interconnecting standalones):**
Dirty Talk | | Dirty Laundry | | Dirty Deeds

Bennett Boys Ranch:
Buck Wild

Connect with Lauren Landish.
www.laurenlandish.com
admin@laurenlandish.com

facebook.com/lauren.landish

twitter.com/laurenlandish

instagram.com/lauren_landish

Made in the USA
Columbia, SC
12 September 2018